"There Will Be No Other Women For Me, No Other Men For You," Alex Said In A Low Rough Voice.

His comment caught her off guard. She would never consider being with another man. Now that she'd been with him, how could she think of anyone but Alex?

"Do you understand?" he asked, lacing his long fingers with hers.

"Of course."

"I take my wedding vows very seriously, Mallory. I'm committed to you," he said.

She nodded, but her mind was still full of questions. The biggest was would he ever love her?

"I'm your husband," he said, his hands moving over her buttons, releasing them with a speed that surprised her. "Soon enough, there won't be an inch of you that doesn't know that you are my wife."

Dear Reader,

You first met wealthy, charming and heartless Alex Megalos in *Bedded by the Billionaire*. Ever met a man with so much charm and good looks he should wear a caution sign? That's our Alex.

You can't blame our heroine, heiress Mallory James, for falling under his spell on sight. Who wouldn't? After she embarrasses herself with him, however, she pulls herself together and declares him out of her league.

When Alex comes around again, she's forced to reject him repeatedly. Alex is determined, though, and with each repeated exposure, Mallory becomes more susceptible to his seductive charms. There's more to him than she'd originally thought. With a man like Alex, it's easy for a woman to lose her head and her heart. But what are his real motives?

Danger: shocking scandals ahead.

Don't you love a delicious, shocking scandal…as long as you're not in the middle of it? Enjoy this newest BILLIONAIRES CLUB story. Another is on the way. After you read this story, visit me at www.leannebanks.com and tell me who you think our next hero will be.

Until next time…

Warmly,

Leanne

LEANNE BANKS

BILLIONAIRE'S MARRIAGE BARGAIN

Published by Silhouette Books

America's Publisher of Contemporary Romance

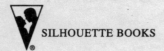

SILHOUETTE BOOKS

ISBN-13: 978-0-373-76886-8
ISBN-10:   0-373-76886-9

BILLIONAIRE'S MARRIAGE BARGAIN

Visit Silhouette Books at www.eHarlequin.com

Printed in U.S.A.

LEANNE BANKS

is a *New York Times* and *USA TODAY* bestselling author who is surprised every time she realizes how many books she has written. Leanne loves chocolate, the beach and new adventures. To name a few, Leanne has ridden on an elephant, stood on an ostrich egg (no, it didn't break), gone parasailing and indoor skydiving. Leanne loves writing romance because she believes in the power and magic of love. She lives in Virginia with her family and her four-and-a-half-pound Pomeranian named Bijou.

This book is dedicated to Tami. Thank you.

One

"She needs a husband."

Alex Megalos looked at the man who had made the statement, sixty-year-old Edwin James, owner of the extremely successful James Investments and Wealth, Inc. Alex wondered if Edwin was hinting that Alex should take on the job.

Alex had successfully avoided commitment his entire thirty years, although things with his most recent girlfriend had gotten a bit dicey and that relationship was headed for the end. The fact that it didn't bother him made him feel a little heartless, but he knew it was best to end a relationship that was doomed. Plus he'd known enough women to realize that they all wanted something. As far as he was concerned, love was fiction in its purest form.

He swallowed a sip of Scotch and glanced across the ballroom at the woman under discussion. A sweet brunette with ample curves, Mallory James was no man-eater like most of the women Alex dated. She wore a modest deep-blue cocktail dress that cradled her breasts, and featured a hem that swung freely at the tops of her knees. Nice legs, but what appealed most about her was her smile and laughter. So genuine.

"Mallory should have no trouble finding a husband. She's a lovely girl with a lot of charm."

Edwin set his empty squat glass on the bar and frowned. "On the outside. On the inside she's a pistol. Plus, she's picky."

Alex did a double take. "Mallory?" he said in disbelief.

"Her mother and I have tried to match her up with a half-dozen men and she passed on all of them. I had some hope for that Timothy fellow she's with tonight, but it doesn't look good. She says he's a great *friend*."

Alex nodded. "Friend. The kiss of death. Just curious. Why do you want her to get married?"

"She's out of college and she wants to work in my company."

"Is that bad?"

Edwin glanced from side to side and lowered his voice. "I hate to admit it, but I can't handle it. She could be a perfect employee but I can't handle the possibility of having to correct her, or worse yet, fire her. The truth is when it comes to my daughter, I'm a marshmallow. You can't be soft if you want to achieve what I have."

"No, you can't. You think marriage will solve things."

"I want her safe, taken care of. She works with a bunch of charity foundations, but she says she wants more. If she's not kept occupied, I'm terrified she'll end up like some of her peers. In jail, knocked up, on a nude sex tape."

Surprised, Alex looked at Mallory again, a wicked visual of her dressed in skimpy lingerie coming out of nowhere. "You really think she's that kind of girl?"

"No. Of course not. But everyone can have a weak moment," he said. "Everyone. She needs a man who can keep her occupied. She needs a challenge."

Alex was at a rare loss as to how to respond. He had approached Edwin to casually set up a meeting to discuss finding an investor for his pet resort project. "I'd like to help, but—"

"I understand," Edwin quickly said. "I know you're not the right man for Mallory. You're still sampling all the different flowers out there, if you know what I mean," he said, giving Alex a nudge and wink. "Nothing wrong with that. Nothing at all. But," he said, lifting his finger, "you may know someone who would be right for my Mallory. If you know some men with the right combination of drive and character, send them my way and I would be indebted to you."

Alex processed Edwin's request. Having Edwin in his debt would put Alex in a better position of strength in gaining the funding he wanted. One of the first rules of wealth was to use other people's money to achieve your goals.

Alex glanced at Mallory. It wouldn't hurt anyone to help Edwin in this situation. In fact, all parties stood to gain.

He caught Mallory's eye and shot her a smile. She gave a slight smile then her gaze slid away and she waved to her father. "I haven't had a chance to talk with Mallory in a while. I'll go over and get reacquainted. I'll see what I can come up with for you, Edwin."

Over six feet of pure masculine power, with dark brown hair and luminescent green eyes that easily stole a woman's breath, Alex Megalos turned women into soft putty begging for the touch of his hands. His sculpted face and well-toned body could have been cut from marble for display in a museum. He was intelligent, successful and could charm any woman he wanted out of her clothes. His charm belied a sharp and tough businessman. As a hotshot VP for Megalos De Luca Resorts, International he was prized for his dynamic innovative energy and making things happen.

So why was he looking at her? In the past, Mallory had always felt he'd looked through her instead of at her. When she'd first met Alex, she'd turned into a stuttering, clumsy loon every time he'd come close. He was so magnetic she'd instantly developed a horrible crush and flirted with him.

And that awful night when she'd actually tried to seduce him… Mallory cringed. Even though Alex had been chivalrous by catching her so she didn't get a concussion from falling on the floor when she'd blacked out, it had been one of the most mortifying moments of her life. Although Alex had thought her fainting spell had been due to her drinking her cocktails too quickly, the incident had been a wake-up call.

Good sense had finally prevailed. She was over the crush now. She knew good and well he was out of her league. Plus she wasn't sure Alex Megalos had the ability to stay focused on one woman for more than a month. Talk about an invitation to heartbreak.

Mallory exhaled and turned toward some guests of the charity event she'd planned. "Thank you so much for coming, Mr. and Mrs. Trussel."

"You've done a marvelous job," Mrs. Trussel, a popular Las Vegas socialite raved. "The turnout is so much better this year than last year. I'm chairing the heart association's event. I would love to get together with you to hear some of your ideas."

"Give the poor girl a break," Mr. Trussel, a balding attorney said. "She hasn't even finished this project."

"I feel like I need to call dibs." Mrs. Trussel

paused and studied Mallory for a long moment. "You aren't married, are you?"

Mallory shook her head. "No. Too busy lately."

"I have a nephew I would like you to meet. He's earned his law degree and been working for the firm for the last year. He'd be quite a catch. May I give him your number?"

Mallory opened her mouth, trying to form a polite *no*. If she had one more setup, she was going to scream. "I—"

"Mallory, it's been too long," a masculine voice interrupted.

Her heart gave a little jump. She knew that voice. Taking a quick, little breath, determined not to embarrass herself, she turned slowly. "Alex, it has been a while, hasn't it? Have you met Mr. and Mrs. Trussel?"

"As a matter of fact, I have. It's good to see you both. Mrs. Trussel, you look enchanting as ever," he said.

Mrs. Trussel blushed. "Please call me Diane," she said. "We were just saying what a wonderful job Mallory has done with the event tonight."

"I have to agree," Alex said. "Would you mind if I steal her away for a moment?"

"Not at all," Mr. Trussel said, ushering his wife away.

"I'll be in touch," the woman called over her shoulder.

As soon as they left, Mallory turned toward Alex. "If you're being nice to me because my father asked you to, it's not necessary."

Alex narrowed his eyes a millimeter. "Why would you say that?"

Mallory moved a few steps away to keep check on the crowd milling through the giant ballroom. She noticed Alex stayed by her side. "Because you were talking with him just a few minutes ago and I know he's trying to make sure I get more friends so I don't move back to California."

"California?" Alex said. "He didn't mention that. Besides, why wouldn't I want to come say hello to you on my own? We've met before."

"Just a couple of times," she said.

"I can even tell you that the first time we met you spilled wine on me." He lifted his lips in a sexy smile designed to take the sting out of his words.

He would remember that. Mallory tried very hard not to blush. She looked away from the man. He was just too damned devastating. "I didn't spill wine. The server did. Even Lilli De Luca said the server was moving too fast."

"That's right. You're good friends with Lilli. Have you seen her and Max's baby?"

"All the time. Even though she has a mother's helper, she lets me take care of David sometimes. Such a sweetheart. He's sitting up on his own now."

Fearing she wouldn't be able to sustain her airy, you-don't-impress-me act much longer, she took a step away from Alex. "Great seeing you," she said. "Thank you for coming to the event tonight. Your donation and presence will mean a lot to inner-city children and their parents." She lifted her hand in a gesture of goodbye. "Take care."

Alex wrapped his hand around hers. "Not so fast. Aren't you going to thank me for rescuing you?"

Her heart tripping over itself at his touch, she looked at him in confusion. He wasn't talking about the time she'd blacked out, was he? "Rescuing me? How?"

"I've met the Trussels' nephew. Nice guy, but boring as the day is long."

Mallory bit the inside of her lip. "That could just be your opinion. Not everyone has to be Mr. Excitement. Not everyone drives race cars in their spare time. Not everyone keeps three women on the string at one time while looking for number four."

Alex's narrowed his eyes again. "I believe I've just been insulted."

Mallory shook her head, wishing she'd been just a teensy more discreet, but Alex seemed to bring out lots of unedited thoughts and feelings. "I was just stating facts."

"You should get your facts straight. Yes, I've had a few girlfriends, but I generally stick to one at a time unless I make it clear that I'm a free agent and the women should be, too."

A few girlfriends. Mallory resisted the urge to snort. "It's really none of my business. Again, I do appreciate your presence and—"

"You keep trying to dismiss me. Why? Do you dislike me?" he asked, his green gaze delving into hers.

Mallory felt her cheeks heat. "I—I need to watch over the event. The headline entertainer will be appearing in just a few minutes."

"Okay, then let's get together another time."

She stared at him for a full five seconds, almost falling into the depths of his charisma then shook her head. Those were the words she'd dreamed of hearing from him eight months ago. Not now. "I'll check my—"

"Hey, Mallory. You're looking hot tonight," a man said in a loud voice.

Mallory glanced at the man with the bleached-blond shock of hair covering one of his eyes as he sauntered toward her. She braced herself. "Oh, no."

"Who is he?" Alex asked.

"Brady Robbins. He's the son of one of the resort owners. He wants to be a rock star and was hoping my father would underwrite his dream. Bad setup," she whispered. "Very bad setup."

"Hey, babe," Brady said, putting his arm around Mallory and pulling her against him. "We had a great time taking that midnight swim in the pool that night. You were so hot. I couldn't get enough of you. Tell me you've missed me?"

Mallory felt her cheeks heat. She'd worn a swimsuit and nothing hot had happened. She tried to push away from him. "I've been so busy," she said, disconcerted by Brady's ability to hold her captive despite his tipsy state.

"The lady's not interested. Go sober up," Alex said, freeing Mallory in one sure, swift movement.

Brady glanced up at Alex and frowned. "Who are you? Mallory and I have a history," he said and tried to reach for Mallory again. Alex stepped between them.

"She doesn't want to share a future with you," Alex said.

"She didn't say that to me," Brady said in a loud voice. "You don't know it, but she has a thing for me. She likes musicians."

Mallory cringed at the people starting to stare in her direction. She didn't want this kind of situation taking the focus off the purpose of the event. She cleared her throat. "Brady, I don't think we're right for each other," she began.

"Don't say that, baby," he said, lunging for her.

Alex caught him again. "Come on, Brady. It's time for you to leave," he said and escorted the wannabe rock star from the room. Mallory said a silent prayer that she wouldn't have to face either man again.

A week later, Mallory's Realtor friend, Donna Heyer, took her to view a condominium at one of the most exclusive addresses in Vegas. The facility boasted top-notch security, luscious grounds with pools, hot tubs, tennis courts and golf courses.

"I love it. Let me see what I need to do to make it happen," Mallory said after they left the spacious condo available for lease. The truth was she would love a closet at this point, as long as she wasn't under the same roof as her loving, but smothering father.

"Just remember," Mallory said as they walked toward the bank of elevators. "This is top secret. I don't want anyone to know, because if my father figures out that I'm determined to move out, he'll have a cow and find a way to sabotage me."

"No one will hear it from me," said Donna, a discreet forty-something woman whom Mallory had met through charity work. "I'm surprised he doesn't understand that you need your independence."

Mallory sighed. "He's afraid I'll turn all wild and crazy."

Donna gasped. "But you would never—"

"I agree I would never, but within the last year, he has developed high blood pressure and an ulcer. When I told him I wanted to move back to California, he had an episode that sent him to the hospital, so I hate—" The elevator doors whooshed open and Mallory looked straight into the green gaze of Alex Megalos. Her stomach dipped. *No, not now.*

"Mallory," he said.

"Alex," both she and Donna chimed at the same time. So Donna knew Alex, too. That shouldn't surprise her. Didn't everyone in Vegas know who Alex was? He was constantly featured in both the business and social pages. Glancing at Donna as she entered the elevator, she bit her lip.

"Good to see you, Donna," Alex said then turned to Mallory. "If you're considering buying here, it's a great property."

"Just looking," Mallory said.

Donna shot Mallory a weak smile that was more of a wince. "I sold the penthouse to Alex."

"Oh," Mallory said, unable to keep the disappointment from her voice. If Alex mentioned it to her father... The elevator dinged its arrival to the street floor and the doors opened. "Donna, could you give me just a second to talk to Alex?"

"No problem," Donna said. "I'll wander around the lobby."

Dressed in a perfectly cut black suit with a crisp white shirt and designer tie, Alex looked down at her expectantly. "You wanted to apologize for not getting back to me?" he said, more than asked.

"Sorry. I've been busy and I knew you would be, too," she said, catching a whiff of his cologne.

"Shopping for a new condo," he said.

"About that," she said, lifting her index finger. "I would really appreciate it if you could keep that on the down low for me. Please," she added.

"You don't want your father to find out," he said.

"At this rate, I'll be lucky to get out of the house by age thirty."

His lips twitched. "You could always get married."

She rolled her eyes. "Ugh. You sound like him. Besides, think about it, what would you have done if your father insisted you get married at age twenty-five in order to move out of the house?"

"Point taken, but you're female. My father would have done the same if he'd had daughters."

"But you can't really agree with the philosophy?" she asked, unable to believe he would share such a point of view. "You're more modern and liberated than that, aren't you?"

"In business, I am. I have to be. But my father is Greek. I was raised to protect women."

She gave him a double take. "Protecting them? Is that what you call what you do?"

He threw back his head and laughed. "Let's discuss this in the car. I can drop you off at home then go to my dull meeting where I have to deliver a speech."

"If you're the speaker, I'm sure it won't be dull. You don't need to take me home. Donna will drop me off at the mall where I parked my car."

He lifted his eyebrows. "This sounds like a covert OP. I can drop you off at the mall. Before you say no, remember you owe me."

"I don't owe you," she said, scowling.

"I helped you ditch your wannabe rock star ex-boyfriend."

"He was never my boyfriend," she told him. "Just a bad setup."

"Yet you took a midnight swim with him and he describes the evening as very hot."

"Probably because he doesn't remember it. If you must know, he had too much to drink and I had to get home on my own."

"I'm beginning to understand why your father wants to keep you locked up."

Alex helped Mallory into his Tesla Roadster, noticing the diamond anklet dangling from her ankle. She wore sandals with heels and her toenails were painted a wicked frosty red. She had nice ankles and calves. Her hips were lush, her breasts even more lush. Her body was more womanly than that of any woman he'd dated, but there was something about her spirit, the sparkle in her personality that got his attention. Despite the fact that women often described him as charming, he'd been feeling old and cynical lately.

"You must exercise," he said as he slid into the leather driver's seat and nudged the car into gear.

"Yes. Why?"

"You have great legs," he said, accelerating out of the condominium complex.

"Thank you," she said and he heard a twinge of self-consciousness in her voice. "I walk and I've started doing Zumba and Pilates. Now back to the discussion about my father, I really would like your promise that you won't discuss my visit to this complex with him."

"I don't see why he needs to know. You haven't taken any action yet, have you?"

"No, but I hope to." She skimmed her fingertip over the fine leather seat. "I wanted this car. It's sporty and green. Once my father read that it goes from zero to one hundred in four seconds, he freaked out. I should have started out telling him I planned to get a motorcycle. Maybe then he would have agreed."

Alex laughed. "You really are trying to drive him crazy, aren't you?"

"Not at all. I just want to live my life." She looked up at the roof. "Can we lower the top?" She glanced at him. "Or are you afraid of messing up your hair?"

He felt a jerk in his gut at the sexy challenge in her words. "I can handle it if you can," he said and pressed the button to push back the roof.

Mallory lifted her head to the sun and tossed back her hair. The sun glinted on her creamy skin and his gaze slid lower to the hint of cleavage he saw in her V-neck blouse. Alex was beginning to get a peek at the wild streak her father had mentioned. He wondered how deep that streak went.

"What do you do with your time?" he asked.

"Plan charity events, volunteer at the hospital and the women's shelter, visit friends, steal away to the beach when I can." She hesitated. "I'll tell you more if you promise not to tell my father."

"You have my word as a gentleman."

"I don't often hear you described as a gentleman," she said.

He threw her a sideways glance. "What do you hear?"

"Lady killer," she said. "Player."

"And what do you say?"

"I don't know you well enough," she said. "I just know I'm not in your league."

He shot her another quick glance. "Why not?"

"I'm not a model or a player. I'm just—" She shrugged. "Me. Average."

"You're far from average."

"Yeah, yeah," she said, waving aside his compliment.

Her dismissal irritated him. "I gave you my word. Now tell me your secret."

"I'm working on my master's degree online."

"What's so bad about that?"

"My father wants me to get married." She lifted her hand. "Take this exit for the mall, please. Oh, and my other secret is that I'm learning to play golf. Now that's funny."

"I'd like to see it."

She shook her head. "No, no. You probably have a handicap of something outrageously good, like ten."

"Nine, but who's counting," he said.

She laughed and shook her head again. "I'm sure you are." She glanced outside the window. "I'm parked near Saks. The white BMW."

He pulled beside the brand-new model luxury car. "That's not a shabby ride," he said.

Opening the door, Mallory turned to stroke the leather seat. "But it's not a Tesla," she cooed.

Amused by her enthusiasm for his car, he couldn't help wondering about her enthusiasm in bed with the right man who could inspire her.

She leaned toward him. "Now, remember you promised you wouldn't discuss any of this with my father."

"I won't say anything."

Her lips lifted in a broad smile so genuine that it distracted him. "Thanks," she said. "I'll see you around." She got out of the car.

"Wait," he called after her.

Turning back, she leaned into the car. "What?"

"Meet me for lunch," he said.

She met his gaze for several seconds of silence then wrinkled her brow in confusion. "Why?"

Alex's usually glib tongue failed him for a half-beat. "Because I'd like to see you again."

"Aren't you involved with someone?"

"No. I broke up with her."

Mallory's eyes softened. "Poor girl."

"Poor girl? What about me?"

She waved her hand. "You're the heartless player."

"Even players need friends," he said, trying to remember the last time he'd had to work this hard to persuade a woman to join him for lunch, for Pete's sake.

She looked at him thoughtfully. "So you'd like me to be your friend." She sighed. "I'll think about it."

Damn it. Negotiations were over. Time for hardball. "Lunch, Wednesday, one o'clock at the Village Restaurant," he said in a voice that brooked no argument.

Her eyes widened in surprise. Her mouth formed a soft O. "Okay," she said. "See you there."

He watched her whirl around, her hips moving in a mesmerizing rhythm as she sashayed to her white BMW. He hadn't realized that Mallory James could be such a firecracker.

If he was going to help poor Edwin find Mallory a husband, he needed to get some more questions answered. Mentally going through his list of acquaintances, he dismissed the first few men as contenders. Whoever he recommended for Mallory would need to be able to stay one step ahead of her. Otherwise, she would leave him eating her dust.

Two

Alex adjusted his tie as he returned to his office after a series of meetings that had begun at seven this morning. His conscientious assistant, Emma Weatherfield, greeted him with messages. "Three calls from Miss Renfro," she said in a low voice.

He nodded because he'd expected as much after he'd broken off with Chloe last week. "I'll take care of it."

Emma nodded, keeping her expression neutral. That was one of the many qualities he liked about his young assistant. She was a master of discretion.

"Ralph Murphy called. I asked him the purpose for his call and he wanted to know if Megalos-De Luca was still acquiring any additional luxury properties."

Alex's interest inched upward. If Ralph, a minor competitor, was calling him, then maybe he wanted to sell. Alex smelled a bargain. "I'll call him before I take lunch. Anything else?"

Emma flipped through the message slips. "Rita Kendall wants you to attend a benefit with her, and Tabitha Bennet wants to meet you for drinks on Thursday. Chad in marketing wants five minutes with you to get an opinion on a new idea." She paused. "Oh, and Mallory James called because she can't make lunch today. She sends her apologies."

Alex stared at Emma in disbelief. "Mallory ditched our lunch date?" He had women practically crawling over broken glass to be with him and Mallory had blown him off. His temper prickled. "Did she leave an alternate day? Did she offer an excuse?"

Emma gave him a blank look and glanced at the message again, shaking her head. "I'm sorry, sir. She was only on the line for a moment and was very polite, but—"

He waved his hand. "Never mind." He took the messages and turned toward his office then stopped abruptly. "On second thought, get Mallory's cell number and find out what her schedule is for the next few days, day and night."

Mallory had been certain Alex Megalos would forget about her after she canceled their lunch meeting. After all there was always a line of ready and willing females begging for his attention. Mallory knew better than to spend any more time with him. He was too seductive and she was too susceptible. He might as well have been the most decadent chocolate she'd never tasted. Truth told, he was the perfect man for an exciting fling, but he'd said he wanted to be friends. It wouldn't take much time with him for her to turn into a pining sap again.

Stunned when he called and left a message on her cell, she procrastinated in responding, not sure what to say. Between her undercover classwork for her online master's degree, her charity obligations and quest to move out of the house, she was too busy for Alex, anyway. He was the kind of man who would take up a lot of space in a woman's life.

She'd agreed to fill in as head greeter for a charity event organized by one of her friends on Saturday night. As guests entered the ballroom event with music flowing from a popular jazz band, Mallory checked off reservations and directed staff to guide the guests to assigned tables.

As the last of the guests arrived, she tidied up the greeter table and tossed out the trash, still undecided whether she would remain much longer. She was tired and she needed to begin work on a research paper.

Glancing at the crowd of people and the beautiful display of flowers, she wavered in indecision.

"Room for one more?" a smooth male voice asked from behind her.

Fighting the havoc that his all too familiar voice wreaked on her nervous system, she whirled around. "Alex," she said in surprise.

Dressed in a dark suit that turned his eyes a shade of emerald, he pointed to the sheaf of paper on the table. "Isn't my name on the list?"

"Well, yes, but—" She'd noticed his name, but she'd assumed he wouldn't attend. Alex's name was always on the guest lists for these events. He was a high-profile businessman and bachelor. Every hostess wanted him at her party. She swallowed over a nervous lump in her throat and glanced at the seating chart. "There are two reserved seats on a front table just left of center. Will that work?" She waved toward the staff escort.

"As long as you join me," he said.

Surprised, she glanced behind him, searching for a woman. "You don't have a date?"

"I was hoping you would take pity on me," he said, but he reminded her of a sly wolf ready to raid the henhouse.

She gave an involuntary shiver of response. "I hadn't decided if I was going to stay for the entire event."

"Then I'll decide for you," he said and took her hand in his.

Mallory stuttered in response but was so caught off guard she couldn't produce an audible refusal. As Alex led her to the front table, she felt hundreds of eyes trained on her and Alex. Alex may have been accustomed to this kind of attention, but she was not. She quickly took the seat he pulled out for her.

The combination of the rhythm and blues band playing sexy songs of want and longing, the warm flickering candlelight and the close proximity of Alex's chair to hers created a sensual atmosphere. Two glasses of wine appeared for them in no time.

He lifted his glass and tilted it toward her. "To time together," he said. "Finally."

He stretched out his long legs and she felt the brush of his leg against hers underneath the table. He glanced at her again with those lady-killer green eyes of his and her chest tightened. She instinctively rubbed her throat and saw his glance fell to her neck and then to her breasts before he met her gaze again.

"You like this band?" he asked.

Forcing her gaze from his, she looked up at the stage and nodded. "The music is moody and the lyrics are—" She searched for the right description.

"Sexy."

The way he muttered the single word made her whip her head around to look at him. He was staring at her, studying her, considering her. She felt a rush of heat and took a quick sip of wine. "Yes," she said. "Do you like them?"

"Yes. Looks like the dancing has started. Let's go," he said and stood.

She blinked at him and remained seated. "Um."

He bent down and whispered in her ear. "Come on, we can talk better on the dance floor."

Confused, she followed him and slid into his arms. Why did they need to talk? she wondered. For that matter, why did they need to be together at all?

"How is your online class going?"

"Good, so far," she said, catching a whiff of his yummy cologne. "But I need to begin a research paper. That's why I was considering leaving early tonight."

"I'm glad I caught you," he said with a hint of predatory gleam in his eyes. "You're a difficult woman to catch. Do you treat all men like me? Blow off lunch dates, don't return calls…"

Embarrassed and then contrite that she'd been rude, she shook her head. "I'm sorry. I didn't mean to be inconsiderate. I just didn't take your invitation seri—" She broke off as his eyes narrowed and she realized her apology wasn't helping.

"You didn't take me seriously?" he echoed, incredulous. "Don't turn all polite on me now."

She sighed. "Well, you're such a flirt. I just didn't believe you."

"No wonder no man can get close to you. Is that one of your requirements? That whoever you date can't flirt? Sounds boring as hell to me."

"I didn't say that. It's that you flirt with every woman. I wouldn't want someone so important to me flirting with every other woman on the planet."

"Does that mean you want someone with very little sexual drive or appeal?"

"I didn't say that, either. Of course, I want a man with a strong sex drive. I just prefer that his drive be focused on me," she managed to say, but felt her face flaming. "But that's not all. He also needs to be intelligent and liberated enough to encourage me to do what I want to do."

He nodded. "You say you want someone you can walk over, but the truth is you want a challenge. I bet if a man played golf with you and took it easy on you that you'd be furious."

Surprised he'd nailed her personality so easily, she felt another twist of confusion. "This discussion is insane. I'm not looking for a long-term relationship right now, anyway. Just like you aren't," she added for good measure.

"That's where you're wrong. When the right woman comes along, I'll seal the deal immediately in every physical, legal and emotional way imaginable."

A shiver passed through her at his possessive tone and she couldn't help wondering what it would be like to be *the right woman* for Alex. Underneath all his charm, could he ever be truly devoted to one woman?

Mallory caught herself. She was insane to even be thinking about his right woman. Heaven knew, it wasn't *her*. Her thought patterns just proved she needed to create some distance between her and Alex.

She glanced at her watch. "I should help the hostess with the extra collections. You don't mind, do you?"

"If I did?" he said.

"Then because this is for charity, you would be a gracious gentleman and allow me to help the hostess," she said firmly.

"Damn, you're good," he said, admiration and something dangerous flickering in his gaze. Mallory supposed she was imagining both.

She smiled. "Excuse me. Good night."

He caught her before she left. "See me before you leave."

His intensity put her off balance. "I'll try," she conceded because she suspected he wouldn't let her leave until she promised that much. She walked out of his arms in the direction of sanity. She'd manufactured an excuse to get away from him. The hostess probably didn't need help, but Mallory sure did.

Mallory did end up helping the hostess with an assortment of last minute minicrises. Just as she was walking down one of the long halls toward the ballroom from one of her errands, she saw Alex approaching her.

"I had to track you down again," he said. "Why are you so determined to avoid me?"

She swallowed over a nervous lump in her throat. "I'm not—avoid—" She stopped when he lifted an eyebrow in disbelief.

"Oh, Mallory," a woman from the lobby called. "Is that you Mallory? My nephew…"

"Oh, no, it's Mrs. Trussel about her nephew. She's been calling me every other day."

"Come with me," he said, taking her hand and urging her down the hallway.

"Oh, Mallory." The voice grew fainter.

"I should at least respond," Mallory said as Alex tugged her around a corner.

"Did you avoid her, too?" he asked, opening a door and pulling her inside a linen closet.

"No. I called and made my excuses. Besides, you're partly to blame."

"Me? How?"

She pointed her finger at his hard chest. "You're the one who told me he was a total bore."

"I should have let you waste your time with him instead?"

"Well, no, but…" She bit her lip and looked around the small, nearly dark room. "Why are we in this closet?"

"Because this appears to be the only way I can get your undivided attention," he said. "You didn't answer my question. Why are you avoiding me?"

She sighed. "I told you. You're a huge flirt."

"Try again," he said.

She closed her eyes even though it was so dark it wasn't necessary. "Because you have this effect on women. You make women make fools of themselves. I don't want to make a fool of myself again," she whispered.

A heartbeat of silence followed. "Again? When did you make a fool of yourself?"

She bit her lip. "I know you remember that night I fainted," she said. "In the bar."

"You'd just drank your cocktails too quickly. It can happen to anyone," he said.

She took a deep breath. May as well get it all over with, she thought. "When I first met you, I was like everyone else. I thought you were gorgeous, irresistible, breathtaking. I—" She gulped. "I had a crush on you. That evening I was trying to—" She lowered her voice to a whisper. "Seduce you."

Silence followed. "Damn. I wish I'd known that. I would have handled the situation much differently."

"As if it would have mattered," she said. "Stop teasing. You know I'm not your type."

Suddenly she felt his hand on her waist. "I'm getting tired of your assumptions."

Mallory felt as if the room turned sideways.

"I can't tell if you're underestimating me or yourself. Damn, if you haven't made me curious," he said and lowered his mouth to hers.

If the room had been turning sideways before, for Mallory, it was now spinning. His hard chest felt delicious against her breasts, his hands masterful at her waist while his lips plundered hers.

Her heartbeat racing, she couldn't find it in herself to resist this one taste, this one time, this one kiss. With an abandonment she hadn't known she possessed, she stretched on tiptoe and slid her fingers through his wavy hair and kissed him back.

She wanted to take in every sensation, his scent, the surprised sound of his breath, the way his hands dipped lower at the back of her waist and urged her closer, his tongue seducing hers.

His kiss was everything and more she'd ever dreamed all those months ago. Hotter, more seductive, more everything… She drew his tongue into her mouth, sucking it the same way…

He abruptly pulled his head back and swore, inhaling heavy breaths. After a second, he swore again. "Where did that come from? I didn't know you—"

Thankful for the darkness in the closet, she bit her still-buzzing lips. "You didn't know what?" she whispered.

"I didn't know you would kiss like that. Hot enough to singe a man, but keep him coming back for more."

Mallory couldn't help but feel a twinge of gratification. After all, Alex was the master seducer.

He lowered his mouth and rubbed it over hers, making her shiver with want. "You could make a man do some crazy things. Who would have known little Mallory—" He broke off and took her mouth in another mind-blowing openmouth kiss. One of his hands slid upward just beneath her breast.

He nibbled and ate at her lips. "Can't help wondering what else is cooking underneath that sweet-girl surface."

A dozen wicked thoughts raced through Mallory's mind. Wouldn't she like to show him what was underneath? Wouldn't she like to feel his bare skin against hers? Wouldn't she like to get as close as she possibly could to him right now?

In a linen closet, some distant corner of her mind reminded her.

And afterward she would have to face the people outside.

She reluctantly pulled back. "I don't think that finding out what's underneath my sweet-girl surface is in the immediate future."

A moment of silence followed. "Why is that?"

"Because I would never want to have a public affair with you."

"This closet is hidden," he said, so seductively he tempted her to leave her objections behind.

"There will be people outside with questions and speculations. I should leave and then you can follow later."

"Later," he echoed.

"It was your idea to pull me in here."

"You would have rather faced Mrs. Trussel?"

She shifted from one foot to the other. "It doesn't matter. I just know I would never want to get involved with you, especially publicly."

"Why the hell not?" he demanded, his voice and body emanating his raw power.

She fortified her defenses. "Because after it's over,

I don't want anyone saying, 'Poor Mallory. Alex took advantage of her.'"

He gave a chuckle that raced through her blood like fire. "What about the poor guy who gets scorched by your kiss?"

She couldn't help feeling flattered, but she pushed it aside. "I should leave."

"I'll be right behind you," he said.

"I don't want to have to answer questions," she said.

"Then grab a towel and say you're cleaning up a mess."

"And you?"

"I'm making plans for the next time you and I get together."

"I don't think that's a good idea."

"I'll change your mind," he promised, and she shivered because she knew if anyone had the ability to change a woman's mind, even her mind, it was Alex.

The following day, Alex's mind kept turning to thoughts of Mallory. She piqued his interest more than any other woman had in ages. Women had come easily to him. The trademark Megalos features had served as both a blessing and a curse for Alex.

With his older brothers committed to medicine for their careers like their father, Alex had always been viewed as the lightweight because he was determined to pursue gaining back influence in the family-named business.

What his father and brothers didn't grasp was that when the tide was rolling against a man, he had to use everything to fight it off—intelligence, charm and power. Alex had used everything he had to rebuild the influence of the family name in Megalos-De Luca Enterprises. He'd butted heads more than once with Max De Luca, but lately the two had become more of a team and less adversarial.

Max had even expressed dismay over the board's decision not to support Alex's plan for a resort in West Virginia near Washington, D.C. Since Alex had secured legal permission to develop the resort on his own, he was determined to make it a success. He would show the board he knew what he was doing, and in the future they wouldn't fight him.

As an investor, Mallory's father could be important to Alex's strategy. Mallory could be the key to unlocking the door to her father.

Funny thing, though, the woman made him damned curious. He pushed the button for his assistant. "Emma, please come into my office."

"Of course, sir."

Seconds later, she appeared, notebook in hand. "Yes, sir."

"I want you to send flowers to Mallory James for me."

Her eyes widened. "Oh. She's lovely," Emma said. "So polite on the phone."

"Not my usual type," he said.

She paused a half-beat. "Much better."

His lips twitched in amusement. Emma was extremely discreet and rarely expressed her opinion unless he asked for it. "How well do you know her?"

"Not well at all. But she's very personable and gracious. You'd never know that her father could pay off the national debt."

"Send her a dozen red roses," he said.

Emma nodded slowly and made a note.

"What's wrong with a dozen red roses?" he asked, reading her expression.

"It's terribly clichéd," she said. "You're dealing with a different quality of woman with Mallory. Something personal might make more of an impression," she said, then rushed to add, "not that you need to impress her."

Alex thought for a moment as several ideas came to mind. "Okay send her a dozen roses in different colors with a Nike SasQuatch driver and a box of Titleist Pro V1 gold balls."

Emma blinked at him.

"She's learning to play golf," he said. "In the note, tell her I'll pick her up for a round of golf on Tuesday at 7:00 a.m."

Three

Tuesday morning at seven-thirty, Mallory was awakened by a knock on her bedroom door. Groggy, she lifted her head and groaned. She'd been up until 4:00 a.m. finishing a paper for her class.

"Miss James," the housekeeper said in a low voice through the door.

Mallory reluctantly rose from bed and opened her door. "Hilda?" she said to the housekeeper.

"There's a man downstairs and he insists on seeing you. Mr. Megalos."

Mallory groaned again. "Oh, no. Not him. I called his assistant to cancel."

"He's determined to talk to you. Shall I tell him you'll be down shortly?" Hilda asked.

"Okay, okay," Mallory said and closed the door. Thank goodness her mother and father were out of town for a business meeting in Salt Lake City, one of the few times her mother left the house. Otherwise, she would be grilled like her favorite fish.

She padded across the soft carpet to her bathroom. Her hair in a ponytail, she washed her face and brushed her teeth. She thought about applying makeup, fixing her hair and dressing up, then nixed the idea. If Alex saw her au naturel, that should really kill his curiosity.

Pulling on a bra and T-shirt and stepping into a pair of shorts, she descended the stairs where he was waiting at the bottom, looking wide-awake and gorgeous.

"Good morning, sleepyhead. Did you forget our date?"

"I called your assistant and gave her my regrets. I had a late night last night."

"Partying?"

"Ha. Finishing my paper until 4:00 a.m.," she corrected and yawned. "I'm sorry if you didn't get my message, but as you can see I'm not ready for a round of golf."

"We may as well squeeze in nine holes," he said. "You won't be able to go back to sleep, anyway."

Frowning at his perceptiveness, she covered another yawn. "How do you know that?"

"I'm just betting you're like me. Once I'm awake, I can't go back to sleep."

She studied him for a long moment. "You have me at a disadvantage. You've obviously had a full night of sleep."

"So I'll give you a few pointers," he said.

A lesson, she thought, her interest piqued. Although she was already taking lessons, it might be interesting to get another approach.

"Nine holes," she said.

"Until you can do the full eighteen," he said, clearly goading her.

She shouldn't give in to his challenge. Although she was tempted, she absolutely shouldn't. "Give me five minutes."

"A woman getting ready in five minutes?" he said. "That would really impress me."

She smiled as she thought about what her finished appearance would look like. No makeup, ponytail, shorts, shirt, socks and golf shoes. "We'll see," she said and headed back upstairs, feeling his gaze on her.

After Mallory took a rinse and spin shower, slapped on sunscreen and got dressed, she joined Alex as he drove to the golf course. She told herself not to focus on her attraction to him. Even though the sight of his tanned, muscular legs revealed by his shorts was incredibly distracting, she tried not to think about how sexy and masculine he was. She tried not to think about how it would feel to be held in his arms, in his bed, taken by him. She tried not to think about how exciting it would be to be the woman who drove him half as crazy as he drove her. Used to drive her, she firmly told herself.

Mallory knew Alex wasn't a forever kind of man, but she'd always thought he would be a great temporary man, amusing, passionate, sexy. If a woman decided to have an affair with him, she would need at all times to remember not to count on him for a long-term relationship. That would be a fatal, heart-breaking mistake.

Not that she was going to have an affair with him, anyway, Mallory told herself as she teed off. She watched her ball fly a respectable distance toward the hole and sighed in relief.

"Not bad," he said. "Just remember to lead with your hips both ways," he said and he swung his club and hit the ball.

His ball soared beyond hers. "What do you mean both ways?" she asked. "How?"

"First get balanced," he said. "Then lead with your hips in the backswing and the downswing. Get behind me and put your hands on my hips," he instructed.

"What?"

"Don't worry. I'm not going to seduce you on the golf course. Unless you want me to," he said and laughed in a voice that made her feel incredibly tempted.

Gingerly placing her hands on his hips, she felt the coil of power as he swiveled his hips and swung the club.

He turned around to face her and glanced down her body. "It's what women have always known. The power comes from the hips."

She felt a heat that threatened to turn her into a puddle of want, but stiffened her defenses and walked toward her next shot. "Thank you for the reminder."

Alex wondered if Mallory was making all those moves deliberately to distract him. After he'd mentioned the tip about hips, she swung her backside before each shot. When she wiggled her shoulders to stay loose, he couldn't help but notice the sway of her breasts.

"Visualize where you want the ball to go," she whispered to herself, and without fail she would bite her lush lower lip, reminding him of how her lips had felt when he'd kissed her.

By the time they reached the ninth hole, he had undressed her a dozen times. He knew she would be in his bed soon, but since she was Edwin's daughter, he figured he may have to play this one a little more carefully.

After she made her last putt, she turned to him with a smile on her face that made the sunny Nevada day seem even brighter. "Thank you for twisting my arm. This was more fun than I'd imagined."

"If you don't enjoy it, then why did you decide to learn to play?"

"The challenge," she said as they walked toward the clubhouse. "I like to learn new things." She laughed to herself. "And my father thought it was a good way to attract a husband."

"But that's not part of your diabolical plan," he said.

"No. But the golf course *is* where a lot of business is conducted," she said.

"Ah. I'm impressed," he said and he was. "The problem with you trying to do business on the golf course is that men will be distracted by your body."

She shot him a sideways glance. "You're not trying to flatter me again, are you?"

He moved in front of her and stopped. "Whatever is between us is more than flattery. I made that clear the other night in the closet. I can make it clear again."

Her eyes widened and she bit her lip. He lifted his finger to her mouth. "Don't do that to your pretty lips," he said. "Let me take you to dinner."

He watched a wave of indecision cross her face. She hesitated an extra beat before she shook her head. "No. I told you I'm not getting involved in a public situation with you where people could misconstrue that we're involved."

He lifted his hand to push back a strand of her hair that had come loose from her ponytail. "We already are involved."

Her eyes widened again. "No, we're not."

"You're not attracted to me," he said.

She opened her mouth then shut it and sighed. "I didn't say that. But I already told you that I don't want to be known as one of your flavors of the month. Wherever you go, you draw attention, so there's no way we could have dinner without people talking about it or it ending up in the paper."

"You really don't want to be seen with me," he mused and shook his head. This was a first. Usually women wanted to parade him in public at every opportunity. Alex switched strategy with ease. "No problem. We'll have dinner at my condo tonight."

Mallory felt a shiver of forbidden anticipation as she stepped inside the elevator that would take her to Alex's penthouse condominium. She shouldn't have agreed, but the more time she spent with him, the more she wanted to know about him.

And who knew? Perhaps Alex could be a resource for helping her get started professionally. As much as she loved her parents, she craved her independence. She needed to succeed on her own.

The elevator dinged her arrival at the penthouse and she took the few steps to Alex's front door. Before she pushed the buzzer, the door opened and Alex appeared, dressed in slacks and a white openneck shirt. He extended his hand. "Welcome," he said and led her inside the lushly appointed condo.

"This is nice," she said, looking around. Although

Mallory was accustomed to the trappings of wealth, even she was impressed with the architectural design and masculine contemporary furnishings.

"I own a home farther out of town, but this is more convenient during the week," he said as they walked toward a balcony with a stunning view.

"It's gorgeous," she said and closed her eyes for a second. "And quiet."

"I chose it for that reason. After a busy day, I can sit here and let my mind run. It's often my most productive time of the day. I come up with some of my best ideas up here or at my cabin in Tahoe." He waved his hand toward a table set with covered silver platters, fine china and crystal. "I sent my staff away just for you. That means we're on our own except for my full-time housekeeper Jean. She'll take care of cleanup."

Mallory sat down at the patio table and wondered how many other women had sat in this very chair. More beautiful, more sophisticated women determined to capture Alex's heart, perhaps even to marry him.

Her stomach twisted at the thought, so she deliberately pushed it aside. This could very well be the only evening she spent with Alex. She may as well enjoy it.

Alex poured a glass of wine and she studied his hands. His fingers were long, and like everything about him, strong and masculine-looking. She wondered how they would feel on her body. She would bet Alex knew exactly how to touch a woman. A twist of awareness tightened inside her, surprising her with its intensity.

Shaking her head at the direction of her thoughts, she took a sip of wine and latched on to the first subject that came to mind. "You mentioned that your father is Greek," she said. "Your family is obviously part owner of Megalos-De Luca. Do you have other relatives working for the company?"

He shook his head and lifted the silver cover from his plate and motioned for her to do the same. "My grandfather only had one son, my father, who chose to go into medicine. His decision infuriated my grandfather so much that he refused to speak to my father."

"Oh, no. That's terrible," she said. "What does your father think of your career choice?"

He took a bite of the lobster dish the chef had prepared. "He hasn't spoken to me since I dropped out of premed, majored in business and got involved in the family business again. My two older brothers went into medicine and the same was expected of me. Business isn't noble enough. It just pays the bills."

"You and your father don't speak?" she asked in disbelief. "What about your mother?"

"My mother sneaks a call to me every now and then, but she feels her job is to support my father."

"My mother takes a back seat approach to marriage, too. She goes along with my father's whims. I don't think I could do it. I don't want to do it," she said more firmly.

"Maybe if you met the right man…"

Mallory swallowed a bite of dinner and shook her

head vehemently. "The right man will encourage me to follow my own goals and ambitions. Isn't it ironic that your father decided to buck his father's trend? Yet when you did the same thing, he reacted the same way as his father."

"The same thing has crossed my mind more than once," he said in a bitter voice.

Mallory felt a surge of sympathy for him. She never would have dreamed Alex's family had totally cut him off. "That's got to be difficult. What do you do for holidays?"

"Ignore them," he said, his gaze suddenly cool. "What about you? You're an only child, aren't you?"

She nodded, wondering if his estrangement with his family truly bothered him so little. "I begged for a sibling until my eighteenth birthday."

He chuckled. "You finally realized it wasn't going to happen."

She nodded, thinking back to that time in her life when everything had changed. "Everything was different after the accident. My mother changed. My father changed some, too."

Alex met her gaze. "What accident?"

"I was seven at the time. My mother was taking my brother and me with her for a quick trip to a nail salon."

"I didn't know you had a brother," he said.

Her stomach suddenly tightening, she pushed her food around her plate. "Not many people do. It's too painful for either of my parents to talk about. He was two years older than me. His name was Wynn and he was a pistol," she said, smiling in memory. "He was the adventurous one. My father was so proud of him."

"Was," Alex prompted.

"My mother ran a stop sign and we were hit by a pickup truck. All three of us had to be taken to the hospital. My brother took the brunt of the collision. He died in the emergency room. They told me I almost died. They had to remove my spleen and I broke a few bones. I stayed in the hospital for a couple of weeks, ate gelatin and ice cream and got out and wanted everything to go back to normal. But it couldn't. I remember how quiet the house was without Wynn around."

"What happened to your mother?"

"She had a few cuts and bruises. They released her after one night, but she has never been the same. She never drove again and I had to push when it came time for me to get my license. The accident frightened both my parents, and she blamed herself for my injuries. Both of them were, are, terrified of something happening to me."

A thoughtful expression settled on his face. "Now it all makes sense."

"What does?"

"Why your father is so protective," he said. "They almost lost you. They don't want that to happen again."

"But you can't wrap yourself in cotton and climb

into a box because you're afraid something bad will happen," she said.

"*You* can't," he said, his lips twitching in humor.

"I love my mother, but I don't want to live my life that way. I sometimes feel as if every time she looks at me, she remembers losing Wynn."

"That's tough," he said.

She nodded. "It has been. She won't really let me get close to her."

"Maybe she's afraid of losing again," he mused.

"Maybe, but I don't want to make all my decisions based on what could go wrong."

"Caught between being the dutiful, devoted daughter and wild woman hiding underneath it all," he said.

"Parental guilt is a terrible thing," she said with a sigh, taking another sip of wine.

"I don't have that problem," he said.

"What about brotherly guilt?" she asked.

"My brothers followed my father's lead. One of them is a researcher," he said and gave a sly smile. "I donate to his foundation anonymously."

She smiled, feeling as if she'd just been given a rare treat. "You just told me a secret, didn't you?"

"Yes, I did. Don't spread it around," he said, shooting her a warning glance that managed to be sexy, too.

So Alex cared more about his family than he pretended, she realized. He was more complicated than the player she'd thought he was. Mallory wondered what other secrets lay beneath his gorgeous surface.

"I won't tell your secret as long as you don't tell my father about my plan to move out and get a job."

"What will you do if he cuts you off financially?"

She shrugged. "I'm Edwin James's daughter. He's taught me how to invest. I have a cushion. Speaking of employment, do you think Megalos-De Luca could use me on staff?"

He paused for a few seconds, a flicker of surprise darting through his green gaze. He quickly masked it. "I hadn't thought about that. Let me get back to you on it."

"Oooh," she said, shaking her head. "Complete evasion. And I had such hopes."

"You didn't really think I invited you here to interview you for a job, did you?" he asked in a low, velvet voice.

She felt a rush of heat and glanced away.

"Are you blushing?" he asked.

She shook her head. "Of course not," she lied. "Dinner was delicious. Let me take my plate to the—"

"No. My housekeeper will take care of it. You're my guest." He stood and extended his hand. "Let's go up to the second level." He led her up a set of stairs to another terrace. This one featured an outdoor pool, hot tub, bar and chaise lounges.

Sensual music so clear the band could have been

right there on the deck flowed around them. A slight breeze sent warm air whispering over her skin. Looking out into the horizon, she felt as if she could see forever. She drew in a deep breath and felt her burdens and dissatisfaction slip away for just a moment. For just a moment, she felt free.

The moment stretched to two, and because Alex was a man, he didn't feel the need to fill the silence with useless conversation. He hadn't made a sound, but she was aware of him. She knew he stood closer, yet not quite touching her, because his warmth radiated at her back.

"If you sold tickets for this, I would buy a hundred," she said.

"For what? The view?" he asked, sliding his hand down her arm.

"Yes, and the temperature, and the breeze, and the feeling of freedom. Do you feel this way every night?"

"No," he said and closed his other hand over her other shoulder. "But you're not here every night."

"Flattery again," she said, unable to keep from smiling. Even though she knew he was just flirting, she couldn't help but be charmed by him. It had been that way since the first time she'd met him.

"Not flattery," he said. "You need a review." He turned her around and lowered his mouth to hers, taking her lips in a kiss that made her feel as if she were a sumptuous feast.

Sliding his fingers through her hair, he tilted her

head for better access and immediately took advantage. He kissed her like he wanted her, like he had to have her. The possibility threw her into a tailspin.

Her heartbeat racing, she felt a shocking surge of arousal that nearly buckled her knees. She kissed him back and his low groan vibrated throughout her body to all her secret places.

"Say what you want, Mallory, but you make me feel free and hungry at the same time. How do I make you feel?" he asked, dipping his head to press his mouth against her throat.

Another rush of arousal raced through her. She couldn't lie. "The same way," she said, her voice sounding husky to her ears.

"What are you going to do about it?" he asked, but it was more of a dare.

A visual of what she wanted to do scorched her brain. "I don't know," she said. "I thought I had you figured out, but there's more to you than I thought there was."

"It's the same for me," he said, sliding his hand upward to just below her breast.

Mallory sucked in a quick breath. "How am I different?"

"I thought you were a sweet girl, quiet and shy."

"And?"

"And you're sweet, but you're not quiet or shy. You've got a wild streak a mile wide and I want to be there when it comes out."

His fingers grazed the bottom of her breast, making her want him even more. It was a feeling she knew that would roar out of control if she let it. She just wasn't sure she was ready for it.

"So what does Mallory want to do tonight?" he asked.

Her limbs melting like wax, she struggled with her arousal. She wanted to let go, but she didn't want to lose herself to Alex. That would be too dangerous.

She grasped through her brain for something else, something that would give her more time. "Your car," she finally managed to say. "I want to drive your car."

Four

Sweet little Mallory had a lead foot.

She rounded corners and made hairpin turns at breakneck speed. Alex began to understand Edwin's anxiety. If it had been his choice, he would put the woman in a nice, big Buick. Or a Hummer.

"This is wonderful," she said, the wind whipping through her hair. "I love that it only has two gears. I can keep it in second gear all the time. I know there were only seven hundred and fifty models of this car made for this year. Who did you have to bribe to get it?"

"No one. I just had my assistant make a few calls and the deal was done."

"Maybe I could order one and hide it," she mused.

Alex laughed. "Do you really think you could hide a purchase like that from your father? You know he has people watching you 24/7."

She shot him a sideways glance. "He's not supposed to hover," she said. "The agreement is if I keep a low profile on the party scene, then the body-guards must remain invisible to me."

"He'll have my hide when he finds out I let you drive my car like a bat out of hell," he said, but wasn't concerned.

"Bat out of—" She broke off. "And I thought I was taking it easy."

He noticed her skirt flipping around her thighs in the wind and slid his hand over her knee.

She swerved and popped forward. "Oops, sorry," she said, pushing her hair behind her ear. "We should go back."

He slid his hand away, pleased that his touch had flustered her. "I know a place that has a great view not far from here."

"Which way?" she asked. "I have a weakness for a great view."

So did he, Alex thought, looking at her skirt still dancing over her thighs. He gave her the directions and minutes later, she pulled into a clearing on top of a hill that overlooked the Las Vegas strip.

"This is beautiful," she said as she killed the engine and leaned her head back. She inhaled deeply. "I'm surprised you let me drive your car."

"I am, too," he said, reaching for her hand.

She turned her head to look at him. "Why?"

"I haven't let anyone drive that vehicle except me. Sure a Ferrari is more expensive, but I had to wait for that electric roadster for over a year. If you wrecked it—"

"You'd just get another one," she finished for him.

He met her gaze. "True." He sat up in his seat and leaned over her. "So you've driven my Tesla. What do you want to do next?" He dipped his mouth to her luscious, pale neck.

She sighed and he slid his hand over her knee.

"The way you act, I almost think you really want me," she said, turning her lips toward his as he skimmed his mouth across her jaw.

"Almost," he echoed, his voice sounding like a growl to his own ears.

"Like I said, I'm not your usual type," she said, shifting toward him.

"Maybe that's a good thing," he said and rubbed his mouth over her sexy, soft lips. He loved the texture and taste of her. He slid his tongue over her bottom lip.

"But you've dated models, actresses," she protested, at the same time opening her lips to give him better access.

"None of them had a mouth like yours," he said and couldn't put off taking her mouth in a kiss. He slid his tongue inside, tasting her, relishing the silken sensation of her lips and tongue.

She gave a soft sigh and lifted her hands to his head, sliding her fingers through his hair. She massaged his head and welcomed him into her depths. With each stroke of her tongue, he felt himself grow more aroused.

He slipped one of his hands beneath her blouse and pushed upward toward her ample breasts. He touched the side of one of her breasts, stroked underneath. He wanted to touch her all over. He wanted to taste her all over.

He felt her heat and arousal begin to rise. She arched toward him and he knew she wanted more. Giving the lady what she wanted and what he wanted, too, he unfastened her bra and touched her naked breast.

She quivered beneath his touch. Her nipple already stiff, she wiggled against him. Her artless response made him feel as if he would explode.

He continued to kiss her, playing with her nipple and slipping his hand beneath her skirt, closer to her core. Reaching the apex of her thighs, he stroked the damp silk that kept her femininity from him.

"You feel so good," he muttered. "So good." He dipped his fingers beneath the edge of her panties and found the heart of her, swollen and waiting for him.

It was all he could do not to rip off both their clothes and drive into her hot, wet, sweetness. She would feel like a silk glove closing around him.

Groaning, he rubbed her sweet spot until she

bloomed like an exotic flower. She began to pant and it became his mission to take her to the top.

"You're so sexy," he said. "I can't get enough of you." Still rubbing over her swollen pearl, he thrust his finger inside her.

She gasped and he felt her internal shudder of release, her delicious shudder of pleasure. "Oh—Al—" She broke off breathlessly as if she couldn't form another syllable.

She clung to him, dropping her head to his shoulder. Seconds passed where her breath wisped over his throat. Finally she let out a long sigh.

"I don't know whether to be embarrassed or—"

"Not embarrassed," he said, still hard as a steel rod. He closed his arms around her.

"Amazed," she said. "We're not even in bed," she said, awe in her voice.

"We will be," he said. "It's inevitable. I have business at one of our island resorts next weekend. I'm taking you with me."

"Next weekend?" she said, pulling her head from his shoulder to gape at him. "But I have papers and I promised to help at a charitable auction."

"Get your paper done before the weekend and find a substitute, Mallory. I won't take no for an answer."

She opened her mouth to protest then closed it. "It's crazy," she whispered.

"Just the way you like it," he said.

"What if I don't—" She broke off. "What if you

don't—" She frowned. "What if we change our minds and decide we don't want to take this further?"

"We can just treat this like it's an extended date."

"No expectations?" she asked.

"If that's what you want," he said, but he knew what would happen.

Relief crossed her features. "Okay."

He brushed another kiss over her irresistible mouth. "I'll send one of my drivers to pick you up and take you to the airport. My assistant will call with all the details."

She looked at him as if her head was spinning. "That, uh, that might not be a good idea. My father—"

"Don't worry. I'll talk to him," he said.

She blinked. "Talk to him? What will you say?"

"I'll tell him the truth—that we're seeing each other," he said.

"I'm not sure that's a good idea," she said. "He may try to push you to—" She broke off and cleared her throat. "He really wants me to get married and he may try to push you to make a—" She cleared her throat and looked away. "Commitment."

"Mallory," he said, sliding his index finger under her chin. "Do you really think anyone could succeed in pushing me to make a commitment I don't want to make?"

She met his gaze for a long moment. "No. I guess not."

"I can take care of me and anyone else who is important to me. I'll talk to him." The poor woman looked dazed. He took pity on her. "Would you like me to drive back to the condo?"

Relief washed over her face. "Yes. Thank you."

Alex cleared his schedule to meet with Edwin James the following evening. The wily Californian poured Alex and himself a glass of whiskey and stepped away from his desk to a sitting area furnished with burgundy leather chairs and mahogany tables. Edwin's office oozed old wealth, but Alex knew the old man had started with nearly nothing. He'd started his own business, expanded, turned it into a franchise operation and began investing, first for himself then others who paid him handsomely.

Alex knew that he and Edwin had a lot in common. He allowed the older man to start the discussion.

"You told me you wanted to build a resort in West Virginia and you'd like me to find you some backers. Why West Virginia?"

So began the interview. Alex answered all of Edwin's questions with a minimum of spin and an abundance of facts and figures.

"Why did Megalos-De Luca turn this down?" Edwin asked.

"Other than the fact that they're blind as bats, and you can quote both me and Max De Luca on that, they're focusing on expanding in current proven markets."

Edwin nodded. "I would think they wouldn't let you do this on your own. Don't you have some kind of noncompete agreement?"

"I do," Alex said. "But I told them I would walk if they didn't make an exception."

Edwin lifted his bushy gray eyebrows. "So you can play hardball when you want. I like that."

"You're not surprised."

"No," Edwin said. "You don't get as far as I've gotten without being able to read people." He paused for a moment. "I've got three or four investors who would be right for this. I'll get back to you by the end of this week." He rose from his chair and extended his hand. "I look forward to doing business with you."

Alex nodded as he shook Edwin's hand. "Thank you. Same here," he said. "On another subject, you asked me to recommend some men who might interest your daughter."

Edwin's eyes lit up. "You have someone in mind?"

"Yes. Me," Alex said. "Mallory and I are seeing each other."

Edwin stared at him for a long moment. "I already knew that," he said. "I have a couple guys who watch over her. They told me about her driving your car. She lost them on one of the turns." He shook his head. "You're a brave man. Just so you know, I would want to show my gratitude in a substantial way to the man who can get my daughter happily down the aisle."

"That would be down the line," Alex said. "We're

still just getting to know each other. In fact, I have to go to one of our island resorts this weekend and I'm taking her with me."

Edwin nodded slowly. "She loves the beach. Just don't let anything happen to her. She's my little girl."

"She always will be even though she's turned into a smart, adventurous and very capable woman," Alex said. "I wonder where she got that adventurous streak."

Edwin cackled and shook his finger at Alex. "You're a smart one, yourself. Maybe she's finally met her match."

Mallory decided not to join Alex for the long weekend. Staring at her unpacked suitcase, she felt like a wuss. A smart wuss, though, she told herself. Even though Alex was unbelievably hot, had allowed her to drive his car and invited her to go on a weekend adventure with him, she knew he was trouble. She knew she would have a hard time hanging on to her sanity.

Rising from her bed, she paced a path from one end of her room to the other and back again. Biting her lip, she glanced at the small stacks of clothes on the bench next to the suitcase. She'd gathered the items necessary for a trip to an island.

Although deep down, she'd ultimately known that she had no business even thinking about going to a fast food joint with Alex, let alone an island resort, she'd been tempted. How could she not be? She loved the beach.

The fact that she would have Alex's attention away from the glare of Las Vegas shouldn't make her shiver with anticipation. The prospect of walking along a beach with Alex, her hand laced with his, the ocean breeze rippling against their skin. A taunting visual filled her mind of sharing a kiss with Alex under the moonlight with the waves lapping at her toes.

Mallory sighed, looking at the stacks of clothes again. It would take so little. Just a few swift motions to lift and lower them into the designer suitcase. She would be insane to do it. Completely and totally insane.

A knock sounded at her bedroom door, startling her. Her heart jumped into her throat. "Hilda?" she said, knowing it was the housekeeper announcing the arrival of Alex's driver. She went to her door, trying to drum up some mental fortitude. She wouldn't make Hilda do the dirty work. Mallory would calmly tell Alex that she had changed her mind.

Taking a deep breath, she opened the door.

To Alex.

"Ready to go?" he asked.

His eyes met hers and his magnetism hit her like a tidal wave. Her throat closed up and she tried to squeak out the word *no.*

He glanced around the room and his gaze landed on the stacks of clothes and the open suitcase. "Sweetheart, you're running behind," he said, lifting the stacks of clothes in his hands and setting them in the suitcase.

Swallowing over the lump in her throat, she found some semblance of her voice. "I was thinking it would be best if I didn't go."

He searched her face. "You were going to chicken out."

"I was not going to chicken out," she said, automatically lifting her chin. "I was just going to make a wise decision."

He walked toward her and her stomach danced with butterflies of expectation.

"This is your chance to let down your hair. Even your dad has given his okay."

She still considered that miraculous. "Yes, but my mother has freaked out. She said she's too upset to get out of bed."

"It's not as if I'm taking you to some war-torn country."

"Alex," she chided him, but couldn't put a lot of oomph into the emotion because she secretly agreed with him.

"You want me to talk to her?" he offered.

Mallory shook her head vehemently. "No, no, no. You don't have a calming effect on women."

He rested his hands on his hips. "I'm not going to try to push you to do something you don't want to do," he said. "I'll walk down to my car and give you five minutes to join me. But don't blame this one on your parents. Make your own decision," he said and left the room.

Mallory stared after him, her heart hammering against her rib cage. She'd spent most of her life forced to be sensible and ultracareful out of consideration for the most important people in her life.

Alex was right. This was her opportunity to taste a little of the freedom she'd been craving, so why was she stalling? Was it because she was afraid of what he brought out in her? Was it because she was afraid of breaking her hard and fast rule to not fall for him?

Taking a deep breath and telling herself to stop overthinking, she put another stack of clothes in her suitcase. She went to the bathroom and grabbed her travel bag of toiletry items and tossed them into the suitcase. She opened the lowest drawer in her dresser and paused, her hand hovering over the bits of silk and lace that she had *never found the nerve to wear in front of another human being*.

Her door burst open again, startling her. Alex and a big beefy man wearing a chauffeur's uniform stepped inside. "I decided you might need some help," he said and glanced down at her suitcase. "Is it ready?"

"Yes, but—"

"Okay, Todd, you mind closing it up and carrying it downstairs?"

"No, sir," the man said and followed Alex's orders.

Alex met her gaze. "And now for you," he said, moving toward her.

Mallory felt her stomach dance with nerves.

"Where's your passport?" he asked.

"The top left-hand drawer in my bureau, but I can get it," she said.

He opened the drawer, pulled out her passport and flipped through the empty pages. Mallory felt a twist of embarrassment at the lack of places she'd been.

"I don't see a lot of stamps," he said.

"No."

"You don't like to travel?" he asked, turning back toward her.

"I love to travel. I just haven't—" She broke off and squealed as he hauled her over his shoulder and walked out of her bedroom. "What are you doing?"

"Carrying you to my car."

Embarrassed, but oddly thrilled, Mallory bounced against his shoulder as he carried her down the staircase. Hilda stood by the front door wearing an expression of shock and confusion.

"Miss James?" she said, clearly unsure what she should do.

"I'm okay," she said to Hilda. "Just don't tell Mom about this. Alex, I thought you said you weren't going to push me."

"Mallory," he said in a sexy, chiding voice. "This isn't pushing. It's carrying."

When he stopped outside a Bentley and allowed her to slide down the front of him, so that she was acutely aware of his hard, muscular body, Mallory looked into his green gaze and relearned what she'd already known. Alex was trouble.

Five

Mallory flipped through a magazine during the flight to Cabo San Lucas on Alex's private jet. She stole a glance at Alex and tried to push aside her edginess. Alex appeared to be working on a redesign of an existing resort, complete with construction plans and artist's renderings.

"Looks nice," she said.

He glanced up and nodded. "These are for a redevelopment for a resort off the coast of South Carolina. I just bought out a competitor last week. It was a steal.

"And you already have plans?" she asked, surprised because she'd heard so many stories about the drag time associated with construction.

He smiled and at that moment, he reminded her of a shark. "The people I work with know not to drag their feet. Otherwise, they won't be working for me."

She nodded. "I wish I'd brought my laptop. That way I could have done some classwork."

He shook his head and leaned back in his seat. "I want this to be a weekend of total relaxation and irresponsibility for you."

She couldn't swallow her humor. "That's not exactly equitable. You're working now and you'll be working at the resort."

"Briefly at the resort," he corrected her. "I'm delivering a keynote because Max De Luca didn't want to go without his lovely wife, Lilli. She wouldn't go because the baby got a cold earlier this week."

Mallory frowned. "I hadn't heard. Poor thing. I know Lilli refuses to leave David when he's sick. She's very protective."

"As is Max," Alex added and glanced down at the drawings again.

"I like that about him," she said thoughtfully.

"What?" he asked.

"I like that Max is protective of David even though David isn't his biological son."

Alex nodded. "Max is tough. Lilli's made him human."

"You like her?" Mallory asked, feeling a twinge of envy.

"She's a lovely woman on the outside and the

inside. She brought cupcakes to the office for Alex's birthday. I thought he was going to fall over, but he loved it. And the cupcakes were damn good. I tried to talk her into making some for my birthday, but Alex told me to call a bakery. SOB."

Mallory laughed. "Are cupcakes your favorite?"

"Anything baked homemade is my favorite," he said. "I like cookies, cupcakes. My favorite is apple pie with ice cream."

She laughed again. "You just don't seem like the all-American apple pie kind of guy."

"Why not?"

"You're too—" She broke off, feeling heat rush to her cheeks.

"Blushing again?"

"I don't blush," she said.

"No?" he said, leaning toward her and lifting his fingers to her cheeks. "Then what is this pretty pink color I see—"

"A gentleman wouldn't make a big deal out of it," she said.

"You've said I'm not a gentleman. And you like that about me," he said, rubbing his index finger over her lips, sliding it inside against her teeth.

Mallory instinctively opened her mouth and he slid his finger onto her tongue. It was an incredibly erotic moment that came out of nowhere. Her gaze held by his, she curled her tongue around his finger and gently suckled.

Alex's eyes blazed with desire and he pushed aside his papers and pulled her onto his lap. "You like to tempt me, don't you?" he asked her. "I think you want to see how far you can push me."

"You started it," she said, her hands resting on his strong chest and loving the sensation of his muscles. He slid his fingers beneath the bottom edge of her blouse and stroked her bare skin.

"Does that mean you want me to stop?" he asked.

Her heart hammering in her chest, she slipped her hands up to his shoulders. "I didn't say that."

"I can't help wondering what you're like when you really cut loose," he said, lowering his mouth to her jaw and kissing.

Craving more, she lifted her head to give him access to her throat. He immediately read her invitation and responded. She sighed at the delicious sensation of his mouth on her bare skin.

"You will be in my bed," he told her. "It's inevitable."

She felt herself sinking under his spell. She wanted him, but she would be a fool to give him her heart.

Five hours later, Alex had delivered one speech and he would give another one during dinner. After that he could attend to his female guest who had followed his advice to make use of all the resort facilities.

As he changed his shirt and tie for dinner, he returned a call to Todd, his chauffeur/bodyguard.

"What's up?" Alex asked, glancing out the window to the wide beach and blue ocean.

"So far, she went snorkeling, spent a little time in a kayak, drove a Jet Ski. Now she wants to go Para-Sailing."

"What the—" Alex stared out the window this time, looking for Mallory and Todd. "You told her she couldn't do it, right?"

"I did. She wasn't very happy about it. Said you and I were as bad as her father," he said.

"Where the hell are you?"

"At the Rigger Resort," Todd said. "It's about four hotels west of the Megalos complex. I bought her a drink in the Tiki bar to distract her, but I don't think it's going to work."

"Okay, I'll be there in a few minutes," Alex said.

"But I'm your driver," he said.

"I'll be there in five," Alex insisted as he left the suite.

Alex easily commandeered a hotel shuttle and walked into the Tiki bar. He spotted Mallory immediately. Dressed in a scant black bikini that emphasized her curves she wore a joyous smile on her face and her long, dark hair was slick against her back. She was riveting. Blinking, he noticed other men were equally riveted. The land sharks were moving in while Todd tried to push them back.

Alex parted the crowd and stood in front of Mallory. As soon as she recognized him, she jumped from her stool and stopped just sort of throwing her arms around him. "Oops. I don't want to get you wet."

"Hey, baby, you can get me wet anytime," a male voice called from a few feet away.

Alex shot the man a quelling glance that sent a hush over the crowd. Then he turned back to Mallory. "You've been busy."

Her eyes sparkled. "I've had so much fun. Loved the Jet Ski. I definitely want to do that again. And snorkel. And snuba. You said you would take me to snuba. I'm almost ready for deep-sea diving." Her brow furrowed and she leaned closer to him. "The only thing is that Todd here is being a spoilsport. I was all set to Para-Sail, but he nixed it. Now it's too late."

He pulled her to the side. "You don't need to do everything in one day," he pointed out. "We can snuba and Para-Sail tomorrow, together."

She searched his face. "I didn't know if you would be busy tomorrow, too."

He shook his head. "Not a chance. And I want to make sure we get the best Para-Sail group. I won't have you risking your gorgeous body with some fly-by-night company."

Her lips curved in a slow smile. "So *you* were the one who nixed the Para-Sail excursion."

"Damn right," he said offering no excuses. "You can wait one more day and do it tandem with me. That way, you'll always associate the experience with me."

"That sounds a little possessive," she said.

"Does that upset you?" he asked.

A moment of silence passed between them where he felt a fist of longing build in his gut, surprising him with its force. He saw the same dark longing reflected in her eyes.

"No," she finally said.

"Good," he said. "Now put on a T-shirt or a robe or something. You're sending the poor locals into a frenzy."

She laughed with delight. "Omigoodness, if I believed half of what you say, then I would be convinced I'm the most desirable woman in the world."

"By the end of this trip, you will be," he told her and slid his arm around her for the benefit of everyone who was watching. He wanted them to know she was with him. "Any chance you could do something boring like shopping or getting one of those spa treatments women like so much."

Biting her lip, she looked into his eyes and he felt an unexpected jolt. "Am I making you nervous? Am I making the man who drives race cars for fun nervous?" she asked in disbelief.

"I wouldn't use the word nervous," he said.

"Then what word would you use?"

"Let's just say you're keeping me on my toes," he said and gave in to the urge to brush his lips over hers. "I'll see you after the dinner meeting and my speech.

Order anything you want from room service then put on a beautiful dress and get ready for a walk on the beach."

"What if I didn't bring a beautiful dress with me?"

"Then go shopping," he said. "I need to leave. Todd will take you anywhere you want to go within reason," he added when he remembered the Para-Sailing.

Within minutes, Mallory finished her fruity beverage and went back to the hotel. She'd packed some cute dresses, but nothing she would consider beautiful, so the pressure was on to find something. She showered and left the resort, and Todd took her to several recommended shops. Nothing grabbed her, so she returned to the resort and looked through the shops there.

Surprisingly enough, she found a hot-pink silk halter-neck dress with sparkles at the bodice and a few scattered throughout. The shopping goddess was on her side. The shop had the dress in her size.

She took it upstairs and immediately changed into it. She curled her hair and added a touch of exotic eye makeup and lip gloss. Hungry, but too excited to eat, she turned on the television and sat on the bed.

Thirty minutes turned into an hour. An hour turned into two. Restless and wondering what had held up Alex, she turned off the television and walked onto the balcony. She closed her eyes as the sea breeze brushed over her. The sound of the surf soothed her.

If her mind weren't whirling a mile a minute, the sound would lull her to sleep.

She couldn't help wondering what she was doing here in Alex's suite. Yes, the suite featured five bedrooms, four bathrooms, full kitchen, formal dining room and a large living area that offered every convenience imaginable, but she was starting to think she'd lost her mind by joining him.

Inhaling a deep breath in search of calm, she caught a hint of his cologne. She opened her eyes and found him standing in front of her.

"You looked so beautiful," he said, lifting his hand to touch a strand of her hair. "So peaceful."

"The sound of the ocean helps," she said, looking at him, noticing that his tie was askew and his shirt pulled loose. "Everything okay?"

"It could be better. I finished my speech and was leaving the ballroom when my ex came out of nowhere."

Mallory stared at him in shock. "Your ex?" she echoed. "Which ex?"

He shot her a dark look. "Chloe Renfro."

"Oh," Mallory said, recalling a willowy blonde. She felt a stab of jealousy, but refused to give in to it. "How did that happen? Does she live here? Have a place here?"

"No to both. She must have found out about my appearance from someone." He pulled his tie the rest of the way loose. "I knew she was going to have a difficult time with the breakup, but I never predicted this."

"You can't totally blame her for having a hard time getting over you. I mean, if a woman grew accustomed to receiving your undivided attention, it could be pretty difficult when your attention goes elsewhere."

"I never gave her my undivided attention," Alex said. "I made it perfectly clear from the beginning that there would be no strings for either of us. Our relationship was not headed for anything permanent."

Ouch. "I wonder how she knew to find you here." An uneasy thought occurred to her. "Unless you brought her here another time." The image tainted the trip for her so swiftly that she tried to push it aside. "But that's none of my business."

He put his hand on her arm. "Mallory, I haven't brought any other woman here but you."

She exhaled, feeling a trickle of relief. "What did you do about her?"

"I arranged for her to get on a flight back to the States," he said with a grim expression on his face.

It dawned on Mallory that this was the flip side of the positive attention and adoration Alex received. "Do you have to deal with this kind of thing often?"

He shook his head. "Despite your impression, I've grown very selective with my dating partners. Just because I'm photographed with a woman doesn't mean I'm intimate with her." He shook his head and shrugged off his jacket. "Enough. I won't allow this to spoil the rest of our evening."

She watched him pull off his socks and step into a pair of canvas shoes. He extended his hand to her. "Ready for that walk on the beach?"

She smiled slowly and accepted his hand. "Sure, let's go."

They took the elevator down to the lobby. At the luxe lounge, Alex bought her a fruity drink and a beer for himself and excused himself from employees who approached him.

Feeling their curious gazes, Mallory was relieved when they stepped outside. "So much better," she said when her feet encountered cool sand.

Alex kicked off his shoes and left them at the foot of the steps leading to the resort. "Beautiful woman, beautiful night. What could be better? Come here," he said and pulled her into his arms. He pressed his mouth against her and tasted her with his lips and tongue, making her feel delicious.

"Mmm," he said in approval. "More."

Her heart tripped over itself. She pulled back and laughed breathlessly. "After our walk."

"I'm surprised you have the energy after all you did today," he muttered as they walked toward the shore.

"I had some downtime while I waited for you."

"Second thoughts about coming," he said.

"How did you know?"

"I could tell," he said.

Surprised, she frowned at him. "How is it that you read me so easily?"

He shrugged. "It's mostly because I want to," he said. "I watch your face and body for signs. I do the same kind of thing when I'm negotiating. You're just a lot more fun to watch," he said, sliding his hand to the top of her opposite hip.

Mallory couldn't deny how wonderful she felt at this moment. With the ocean beside her, the sand at her feet and Alex's arms around her, she couldn't imagine anywhere she would rather be.

"I had a wonderful time today. Thank you for bringing me," she said, looking up at him.

"You were supposed to say you missed me desperately," he said in a mocking tone.

"Just as you missed me," she said innocently.

"Trust me, you had more fun than I did." He shook his head. "Poor Todd couldn't keep the men away from you. It's a wonder I didn't have to fight off a few of them to get to you."

She laughed. "Would you have really done that?"

"You like that idea, do you?" he asked, squeezing her against him.

Heaven help her, she did, at least in theory. How crazy was it that she was preaching liberation on one hand yet loving it when Alex went primitive on her? She couldn't admit it aloud, though. She heard the strains of beach music coming from a resort up ahead. The romantic sound tugged at her.

Alex came to a stop and swung her against him. "Dance?"

Her heart skipped and stuttered. "Yes," she said and began to follow his lead. "You're a good dancer," she said. "When did you learn?"

"When I was young. It was a requirement in my family. My mother was determined that her sons would be civilized and have good manners. I hated every minute of it until I started noticing the opposite sex. Then I figured out that dancing is a damn good way to get close to a woman you want to get to know better. But there's an even better way," he said, sliding his hand down to the back of her waist and drawing her intimately against him.

He felt so good, so strong, and Mallory was so tired of resisting him. She'd always told herself he was the perfect man for a fling. He brought out a wildness in her and made her feel as if it were okay.

She felt something inside her rip so strongly she could almost hear it. Restraint, resistance, she was impatient with living under her code of caution.

"If you and I get closer," she began, her heart beating like a drum in her chest.

"We will," he said, dipping his mouth over hers and away, revving up her temptation.

"I want to keep it confidential," she said. "Secret."

He paused a half-beat. "You want me to be your secret lover?"

"I don't want my parents hurt by any sort of publicity," she said. "And that's the last sensible thing I want to say."

"Are you ready to go wild?" he asked and lifted the inside of her wrist to his mouth. "You taste so good. I can't wait to taste every inch of you."

"Then don't," she whispered. "Don't wait."

Six

But he did wait, and the waiting just made the tension inside her stronger. Mallory had expected Alex to whisk her back to the hotel and immediately devour her. Instead he continued to dance with her on the beach, taking her mouth in long, drugging kisses that made her knees turn to liquid.

The darkness surrounded them like a cocoon of privacy. No one else was anywhere within sight. She wasn't aware of anyone else. She was solely focused on Alex.

He slid one of his hands all the way up her side to the outer edge of her breast and caressed her from the outside of her dress. She felt her nipple harden from the indirect touch. She craved feeling his skin on hers.

An edginess built inside her. "Shouldn't we go back to the suite?" she asked, biting her lip against a moan as he slid one of his fingers just inside her dress to her bare breast.

"We will," he said. "Trust me. I want to take my time with you. Once we get back to the room and I take off your clothes, it will be hard for me to slow down.

"Your skin feels so soft, so edible," he murmured, dipping his mouth to her throat again.

Her pulse spiked.

"I love the way your body responds to me," he whispered. "When I touch you, you take a little breath and hold it. Is that because you want more? Or less?"

She bit her lip at the sharp wanting he caused inside her. "More," she whispered and boldly pulled at the buttons at the top of his shirt. She splayed one of her hands across his smoothly muscled chest. "I want to feel you, too."

He sucked in a sharp breath as if she'd surprised him. Tipping her head backward, he slipped one of his hands through her hair and took her mouth again. This time his kiss was more aggressive, more purposeful. He slid his thigh between hers, and Mallory's breath just stopped.

Feeling his arousal pressed against her, she reacted purely on instinct, undulating against him.

Alex swore under his breath. "Time to go. But if

this were a private beach," he said, and a shocking visual raced through her mind of Alex, naked and taking her right there. The power of it shook her.

She stumbled as he led her toward the resort. He caught her against him. "Okay?"

Mallory had never been this aroused in her life. Never wanted so much to take and be taken by a man. "Yes. No." She swallowed over the emotion building in her throat, a combination of apprehension and anticipation. "I—just—really—want you."

He met her gaze and she saw the same hunger mirrored in his eyes that she felt in every pore of her body. He took her mouth in a quick, but thorough kiss. "You're going to get me," he promised in a gritty, sexy voice and urged her toward the resort.

As soon as they stepped inside, he took a right down a different hallway. "Let's take the back elevators. I'm not in the mood for small talk with one of my employees."

As if even the elevator knew not to impede Alex, it immediately appeared and Alex pulled her inside. As soon as the doors closed, he took her mouth again, urgency emanating from him.

Dizzy from his touch and the heat he generated inside her, Mallory clung to him as the elevator door swept open. A man stepped inside, giving her a second and third look before he got off the elevator three floors later.

Self-consciousness trickled through her and she closed her eyes.

"Did you know him?" he asked.

She shook her head and met his gaze. "Does it show on my face? How I feel?" she asked. "That I'm so turned on I can't—"

He covered her lips with his finger. "You're not alone," he told her, and the elevator finally arrived at their floor.

Alex led her to the suite and before he'd closed the door, he was pulling her into his arms. "There's something about you," he said in a rough voice. "It must be in your skin, in your voice, deeper. I just know I have to have you. All of you."

Tugging her farther into the suite, he pulled her down on the sofa with him and took her mouth in a consuming kiss that made every cell inside her buzz with need and pleasure.

Skimming one of his hands up her side, he found the side zipper of her dress and pulled it down. With his other hand, he untied the knot of silk at the back of her neck. He pulled the soft, sensual material down, baring her breasts.

She felt a whisper of coolness from the sudden exposure, but the heat of his gaze warmed her. He lifted his hands to her breasts, taunting her already sensitized nipples and she looked away, swallowing a moan.

"Oh, no," he said, putting his hand under her chin

and drawing her gaze back to his. "No hiding," he said. "No holding back. I want to see every look, feel every response, hear every sound you make."

Shoving aside her doubts and insecurities, she reached for his shirt and unfastened the rest of the buttons. "Fair is fair," she said, her heart racing like the wind. Urged on by his gaze and her need to be close to him, she pushed his shirt down and pressed her swollen breasts against his chest.

Her moan mingled with his. She felt the muscles of his biceps tense beneath her hand. He swore and took her mouth in a searing kiss.

In the middle of that endless kiss, he pushed her dress aside and slid his hand between her thighs. With unerring instinct, he found her most sensitive, most secret place.

His groan vibrated throughout her. "You're so hot, so wet," he said, his low voice full of approval and need. "I want you everywhere at once," he said and pushed her against an oversize pillow. He skimmed his mouth down her throat to her chest and then he slid his tongue over one of her nipples. A second later, he drew the aching tip into his mouth and she felt a corresponding twist of sensation low in her belly.

As he stroked her between her thighs at the same time he consumed her breasts, Mallory felt her head began to spin. Tension, need and a wanting so vast it shook her to the core. She felt herself climbing to a precipice. He'd taken her there before in the car. But this time, she didn't want to go without him.

"Alex," she managed to say, pulling herself upward. "I want—" She broke off and swallowed. "I need you to—" Meeting his gaze, she lowered her hands to his slacks and tugged his belt loose. "Inside me," she said in a voice that sounded husky to her own ears.

His eyes nearly black with arousal, he stood, stripping off his slacks and underwear. Transfixed by the sight of him, she stared at his muscular body from his strong, wide shoulders over his well-built chest, flat abdomen and his large masculinity jutting from his pelvis.

His size made her wonder if she was ready for him.

Still watching her, he pulled a packet from his pocket and put on the protection. Then he slowly covered her body with his. She felt his erection between her thighs and everything except being with him fled her mind.

He rubbed against her intimately and she arched to take him inside. Sliding his hand between their bodies, he played with her again. Each stroke made her more desperate for him. "Please," she whispered, but she didn't want to beg.

"Hold on," he told her and pushed her thighs apart and thrust inside her.

His invasion stole her breath. "Alex," she breathed and they began to move in an age-old rhythm of possession and surrender. She could feel how much he wanted her, how much he craved her. It was as if he wanted to capture her spirit and soul to light the darkness in his, and Mallory knew nothing would ever be the same for her again.

The next morning, Alex awakened early as he always did. Propping his head on his elbow, he looked down at Mallory, stretched out on her side with the sheet wrapped around her waist. Her brown hair fell in shiny, sensual waves over the top her chest and shoulders. The sight of her voluptuous bare breasts taunted him. During their multiple rounds of lovemaking last night, he'd noticed how her nipples hardened just by him looking at them. Everything about Mallory's body responded to him.

Her responsiveness seemed to go deeper than her skin, although he sensed she wanted to hold some part of herself back. The more Alex was around Mallory, the more he wanted all of her.

He liked the way she pushed back at him. She didn't need his money, and wasn't at all interested in the notoriety her relationship with him could bring her. Her desire to keep their affair secret amused him at the same time that it pinched his pride. If he decided he wanted more from her, though, he would change her mind. Some might consider him arrogant, but for Alex it was just the truth. It was very rare that he didn't get what he wanted. He wanted Mallory and he intended to enjoy every minute of their secret lover weekend. He would make sure she enjoyed every minute, too, but he would give her a little break, noting the violet shadows under her curly eyelashes. He knew he'd worn her out last night.

Sliding out of bed, he went into the den and called room service for breakfast. The newspaper would be delivered in mere minutes, so he grabbed a quick shower and pulled on a pair of shorts. As expected, breakfast, along with three newspapers, arrived shortly. He directed the staff to set the breakfast on the large wraparound balcony.

If Mallory didn't awaken soon, then he would read the papers and reorder for her when she rose. He'd barely finished his first article from the *Wall Street Journal* when she appeared, wrapped in a fluffy robe with sexy, sleepy eyes, as she peeked from the bedroom sliding doors.

"Good morning," he said. "You're just in time for breakfast."

"There's some for me?" she asked, moving toward the table. "The smell of something heavenly woke me up."

"Coffee?"

"Bacon," she corrected, sitting down in the chair opposite him. "The most useless food on the planet."

"But too good to resist," he said, lifting a slice and offering it to her.

She took it and devoured it, closing her eyes as she

ate it as if it were a sensual experience. He wondered how a woman could make eating bacon so arousing, but damn if she didn't.

"I'm starving. I didn't eat dinner last night—"

He frowned. "Why not? I told you to order anything you wanted from room service."

She met his gaze. "I was a little nervous," she confessed.

Something inside him tugged and twisted at her admission. "The prospect of Para-Sailing didn't bother you, but I did?"

"Oh, being with you is much more—" She broke off. "Much more everything than Para-Sailing. They told me Para-Sailing is over in five minutes."

"I hope I lasted longer than that."

She giggled, covering her eyes. "Oh, wow."

Her response was addictive. He tugged her hand and pulled. "Come here. Have some breakfast."

She sat on his lap with no protest. Surveying the plates he'd ordered, she made a little moan of approval. "I want a bite or two of everything," she said and took a bite of the omelet. "Delicious. Have you ever noticed how everything tastes like gourmet food when you're starving?"

He nodded. "Even a stale sandwich from the deli because you don't have time to get anything else."

"Exactly. But since you're a big whoopty-doo VP, I would think your employees would always make sure you get perfectly fresh food."

"Contrary to rumor, I don't force my employees to work the same hours I do. I sometimes work late nights and have been known to grab a package of crackers from the vending machine."

She made a tsking sound of false sympathy. "Poor big whoopty-doo VP."

"You're heartless."

"That's me, heartless Mallory." She smiled then glanced at the food again. "Oh, don't tell me that's a chocolate croissant."

"It is," he said, enjoying every minute of having this woman on his lap.

She sighed. "I may have to eat more than two bites of that."

He snatched the croissant from the plate. "You may have to kiss me to get it."

She met his gaze with soft, but searching eyes. "I would have thought you'd gotten so many kisses last night that you wouldn't want anymore."

"In that case, you would have been very wrong," he said and took her mouth with his.

Mallory was in beach and man heaven. She'd known Alex's attention could be intoxicating, but she'd really had no idea how intoxicating. Doing snuba, a combination of snorkeling and scuba diving, with Alex, Mallory felt as if she were discovering a whole new wonderland. The vibrant colors of the reefs and fishes were spectacular and joining hands with Alex while twenty-five feet underwater upped the thrill exponentially.

As promised, they Para-Sailed tandem. Surprisingly when they hovered above an inlet, it felt more peaceful than frightening. Alex took her mouth in a kiss that sent her heart soaring into the stratosphere. Every once in a while, she wondered how she could possibly return to her claustrophobic existence after experiencing so much freedom.

After their busy morning and early afternoon, they enjoyed a gourmet picnic lunch on a private beach. Mallory guzzled an ice-cold bottle of water.

"You're turning pink," Alex said, pressing his finger against her arm. "Get under the umbrella. Do you need more sunscreen?"

She moved to the double chaise lounge underneath the umbrella. "I've applied it a gajillion times today."

He joined her on the lounge, his skin gleaming bronze from their time in the sun. "Not exaggerating, are you?"

"No," she said, admiring and resenting his tanned skin at the same time. "It isn't fair that you don't burn."

"My ancestry. I guess it's one thing I can thank my father for," he said with a dry laugh and pulled out a bottle of sunscreen. He poured some cream into his palm then rubbed it onto her shoulders.

"Do you miss him?" she asked after a long moment.

"Who?"

"Your father. I can't imagine not being able to talk to my father whenever I want." The idea actually hurt her heart.

"I've gotten used to it," he said with a shrug, rubbing the sunscreen onto her belly.

"I think that's a lie," she said.

He met her gaze and lifted a brow. "And who made you the expert on me?"

Her heart twisted like a vise and it hit her that she wished she could be an expert on Alex. She wished she could know him in every possible way. "Am I right?" she asked.

He laced his fingers through hers. "You keep surprising me," he said. "One minute you're wild, the next you're deep and thoughtful."

"You didn't answer my question," she said, willing him to meet her gaze. A long silence followed, and she resisted the urge to fill it.

"I miss what could have been. Sometimes the death of dream is worse than a real death." He met her gaze and the naked emotion in his green eyes took her breath and stole a piece of her heart. "Satisfied?"

She wondered if she would ever be satisfied. If she could ever know enough of him and not want more. She rose and pressed her lips to his. It seemed the right thing to do.

When she pulled back, he trailed his finger between her breasts. "You know this is a private beach. There's no one else but you and me here." He slid his finger around the edges of the cups of her bathing suit. "You could take this off…."

Her pulse raced at the invitation in his voice. It was more an invite than a dare. "I've never gone topless on a beach before."

"Have you wanted to?" he asked.

"Not before," she said, but she liked the idea of taunting and tempting him. With his experience, he always seemed to have the upper hand.

"And now?" he asked, sliding his finger beneath the edge of the top of her bathing suit, just a fingertip away from her nipple. She felt her nipple grow hard and fought against the urge to arch against him.

"I could get burned even worse since that skin has never seen the sun," she said, her voice husky to her own ears.

"I would be happy to put sunscreen on you," he said. "Every inch."

Mallory closed her eyes, wondering if she wanted to be this wild, wondering if she could. Still keeping her eyes closed, she lifted her hand and untied the strings at the back of her neck. She pushed the cups down and reached behind to unfasten the other strings at her back, then pulled the top of her bathing suit from her body.

She finally opened her eyes.

Alex gazed at her possessively, his nostrils flaring slightly in sudden arousal. She was surprised, but gratified by the speed of his response.

He met her gaze. "You have no idea how you affect me."

An illicit thrill raced through her. "Maybe you should show me."

He slid his hands over her breasts. "My pleasure," he said.

He taunted her with his hands, then replaced his hands with his mouth. He nibbled at the hard, sensitive tips of her breasts, making her want more and more. He took her mouth in a French kiss and rolled on top of her, pushing her thighs apart.

In the afternoon sun, shielded only by the umbrella, he took her with a glorious, consuming intensity. She reveled in the sound of the waves as he thrust inside her. The scents of salt, sand, coconut oil and musk filled her head. She wanted him to take her. She wanted him to fill her completely and in his taking, she wanted him to feel completely full. It was the most carnal yet spiritual experience in her life, and she wondered how she would possibly survive being separated from him.

The next day, they had to return to Las Vegas. Both she and Alex were quiet. He studied designs and reports. Mallory looked through the same magazine for the fifth time, not seeing a single image, not reading a single word. The weekend had been the most glorious of her life, but she was searching for a way to pull herself together. She'd been stretched sexually and emotionally. How was she supposed to go back to her parents' home and be the Mallory she'd been before? How could she?

Thirty minutes before they were scheduled to land, she sensed Alex looking at her. "I want you to move in with me," he said.

Her heart leaped in her chest. She couldn't. Not for her peace of mind, not for her parents' peace of mind. "I can't do that. Right now," she added.

"Why not?" he asked.

"My parents are old-fashioned. They would be horrified and hurt. Besides, you and I need to be sensible. I told you before I didn't want a public affair." She shook her head. "I need to get my own place. If you still want to see me—" She broke off, floundering.

"Want," Alex echoed, taking her hand in his. "You've given new meaning to the word. You can't believe social conventions are bigger than what is going on between you and me."

Her heart twisted and she met his gaze. "This isn't about conventions. I've got to recover from being with you. I don't want to be one of those women who can't get over you. I'm starting to feel more and more sympathy for them," she said.

"This is different," he said, swearing. "It's wrong for you to not be with me."

Every cell in her urged her to say *yes*. Her connection with Alex had been so powerful it had seemed almost otherworldly. Her brain stepped in like a sharp elbow-jab. Alex was a player. This could be over in a second and she would be picking up the pieces of her heart. By herself. "It's too fast," she said, meeting his green gaze, rocked by the emotion she saw there. "I need more time."

Seven

"You're glowing," Lilli De Luca said, two days later, as she joined Mallory for lunch at an outdoor café shielded by umbrellas. "If it's a new spa treatment, please tell me what it is. My sweet little David is wearing me out with his teething."

Mallory smiled, thinking of Alex. "I took a trip to the beach over the weekend. Maybe you should try to do the same soon."

The waiter refilled their glasses of mint iced tea. Mallory remembered how good the iced bottle of water had felt on her throat the afternoon she and Alex had spent on the beach.

Lilli made a face. "Max and I were supposed to

go to the beach this past weekend, but David got sick and I just couldn't leave him."

"I know," Mallory said then tried to take back the words. "I mean, I heard something about David being sick."

Lilli lifted her eyebrows in surprise. "Really? From who?"

Mallory shifted in her wrought-iron chair. "Um, I think Alex Megalos may have mentioned it."

Lilli's eyes widened farther. "Alex? When did you see him?"

"Oh, he's everywhere," Mallory said, waving her hand. "You know, Mr. Social, in the spotlight."

"Hmm," Lilli said, studying Mallory. "I remember how you used to have a crush on him."

"Most single women do," Mallory said, her stomach tightening. "Probably some married women, too. He's charming, good-looking and sexy," she tried to say in a matter-of-fact voice.

Lilli took a bite of her sandwich and swallowed it. "Is there something you're not telling me that you want to tell me?"

Mallory's throat tightened. "I'm not sure. Off the record, just how much of a hound dog would you say Alex Megalos is?"

Lilli furrowed her eyebrows. "Aside from my husband, he is one of the most charming men I've ever met. He actually hit on me when I was pregnant. Very flattering."

"But you were gorgeous when you were pregnant," Mallory said, pushing aside a stupid twinge of jealousy. "And gorgeous when not pregnant, too."

Lilli smiled. "You're such a good friend." She paused. "Here's the thing. Alex is a paradox. He's a terrible flirt. But do you know what he gave David as a gift? A year of tuition at any college and a Tonka truck he can ride. And get this, Alex made me swear that I would support David if he decided to be a sous-chef instead of a tycoon for Megalos-De Luca. How can you not love him for that?"

Mallory thought of Alex's unrelationship with his own father and tears filled her eyes. "How can you?" she echoed.

Lilli studied Mallory for a long moment. "You're still not telling me something."

Mallory blinked her eyes against the tears. "I've kinda gotten involved with Alex," she confided.

Lilli's eyes widened. "How involved?"

Mallory bit her lip. "Pretty involved. Too involved. I'm scared."

"If he hurts you, I'll kill him. I'll make Max kill him, too."

Mallory shook her head. "No murder needed. He asked me to move in with him."

Lilli stared at her, speechless. It took her a full moment to find her voice. "Move in? As in his house?"

"Or condo," Mallory said. "I told him no. My parents would freak. I don't want to make Dad's blood pressure spike through the roof. And my mother is finally coming out of her bedroom since I spent the weekend with Alex. At the beach."

Lilli shook her head. "One surprise after the other. I always thought there was more to Alex than met the eye. He's so good-looking and charming you're tempted not to look any further."

"And once you do, you're hooked," Mallory said.

"Oh," Lilli said and gave a sympathetic smile. "I don't know what to say."

"Just say you'll be my friend whatever happens," Mallory said, unable to avoid an impending sense of doom about her relationship with Alex. She couldn't imagine being able to hold his attention for long.

Lilli covered Mallory's hand. "Always," she said. "I'm always your friend, just as you've been mine since the first time we met. Just remember, both Max and I will kill Alex if he hurts you."

Twenty-four hours later, Alex called her. "You and I need to meet. There's been a development. Come to my office immediately."

Entrenched in research for her term paper, Mallory frowned into her cell phone. "Development?" she echoed. "That's a little vague. I'm in the middle of this paper. Can't you give me more information?"

"Mallory," he said and she could hear the stretched

patience in his voice. "I won't discuss this on the phone. I'll send my driver to—"

She sighed. "No, no. I can drive myself. Give me an hour."

"Thirty minutes," he countered and hung up.

Mallory stared at her cell phone and felt a frisson of fear. Alex had never sounded like this before. There was an eerie calm to his voice. A chill passed over her and she took a deep breath. Saving her file, she shut down her computer, changed her clothes, applied lipstick and mascara and headed for Megalos-De Luca Enterprises.

A valet attendant greeted her and took her car. Mallory walked inside the skyscraper, and security took her name and immediately allowed her to pass. Alex had clearly prepared everyone for her arrival.

With each passing second, she felt her tension increase. What could possibly be so important that he couldn't discuss it with her on the phone? As she took the elevator to the top floor, she tried to conjure the worst scenario. Her heart sank. If he wanted to banish her from his life, this was an odd way to do it.

The steel elevator doors opened and she stepped outside. She spoke with a receptionist who pointed her toward a corner office. She approached a woman outside the corner office. "I'm looking for Alex Megalos's office."

The young woman nodded. "And you are?"

"Oh, I'm sorry. I should have introduced myself. Mallory James."

The woman smiled. "Miss James. It's nice to meet you. I'm Alex's assistant, Emma. Please go on in. He's waiting for you."

"Thank you," Mallory said and took a deep breath as she opened the door to Alex's office.

Alex looked up, then immediately stood. "Come in. Please close the door behind you."

Mallory did as he asked. "I can't tell if I feel like I've got an appointment with the CIA or the principal from my elementary school."

He didn't smile at her remark. That made her more nervous. "Have a seat," he said.

She gingerly sat in the chair across from his desk. "I'm already nervous and you're not making it better."

"Unfortunately it's going to get worse before it gets better," he said.

Her heart sank further. "I can't stand it, Alex. Just tell me."

"You remember that day we spent on the beach on the island," he said.

She nodded. "We ate and talked and…"

"Made love," he said for her.

She nodded again. "Yes."

"We were supposed to be alone. It was supposed to be private."

She frowned in confusion. "There was no one around."

His eyes turned to chips of green ice. "No one we could see. Someone using a long-range lens took photos."

Shock coursed through. She lifted her hand to her mouth. "Oh, my God. You can't mean…"

"The photographs are grainy, but they've shown up on the Internet."

Alarm turned her blood to ice. "The Internet?" she echoed, trying to comprehend what he was saying. "Our pictures are on the Internet. *We* are on the Internet?"

His face grim, he nodded. "Yes. We're putting together a number of action plans to counter the negative impact of—"

"We?" she said weakly. "Who is *we?* How many people know about this?"

"So far, just the company's top PR official, your father and me," Alex said. "I'll handle this," he said. "I'll protect you."

"How can you?" she asked, numb and humiliated at the same time. "And my father." She shook her head.

"I will," he promised and his phone buzzed.

He picked up the receiver. "Yes, Emma." His face turned more grim. "Let him in."

Seconds later, Edwin James, Mallory's father, walked through Alex's door with murder in his eyes. "You've destroyed my daughter's reputation," he said to Alex. "What kind of man are you to take advantage of a young lady like Mallory?"

"Daddy," Mallory exclaimed.

"I'm going to take care of this," Alex said in that eerily calm tone.

"There's only one way you can do that," her father said.

"I know."

"The two of you have to get married."

Mallory gasped. "That's ridiculous."

Alex met her gaze. "No. It's not."

She shook her head, feeling as if the whole situation had turned completely surreal. "This is the twenty-first century. It's true my reputation may suffer a little," she said.

"A little," her father said.

Mallory's stomach dipped. "This will just be the scandal of the moment. It will pass. There's no reason to make a permanent decision because of it."

"You want people thinking you're some kind of—" Her father broke off as if he couldn't say the words. "Loose woman. You want people thinking you're a—" He shook his head again as if he couldn't stand the very notion of it. "I won't have it. You were a sweet and innocent woman until you hooked up with Megalos here. He's ruined you."

"He hasn't ruined me," she protested.

"There's only one solution to this problem," her father interjected. "You and Megalos need to get married and soon. Now don't argue, Mallory," he said, shaking his finger at her. "Even Alex agrees with me. I just hope I can keep this from your mother. The disappointment would devastate her."

Guilt sliced through Mallory. In this, her father was right. Her mother was fragile. Although Mallory chafed against the constraints her parents had placed on her, she loved them both deeply and hated that she was causing them pain. She bit her lip. "This is such a huge move to make just for the sake of covering a scandal. Neither Alex nor I were anywhere near ready to make that kind of commitment."

Alex moved from behind his desk, his green gaze wrapping around hers and holding tight. "I can't agree with you. You know I'd already told you I wanted you to move in with me."

Her father swore under his breath.

Mallory's stomach knotted. "Did you have to say that in front of him?" she whispered even though she knew her father could hear her.

"This discussion is a waste of time," her father said, pounding his fist on the desk. "The solution is obvious to everyone." He pursed his lips at Mallory. "It should be obvious to you."

Confused and overwhelmed, she looked at her father. "Daddy, could I please have a moment alone with Alex?"

He clenched his jaw. "Seems to me you've had a few too many moments alone with him."

"Daddy," she said in a chastising voice.

"Please, Mr. James," Alex said, surprising Mallory with his support.

"Okay," her father said. "I'll be outside."

"You don't need to go all the way downstairs," Mallory said.

"I need a cigar," he said.

"You're not supposed to be smoking," she called after him as he stormed out of Alex's office. Her heart swirling with a dozen different emotions, she turned to Alex. "This is crazy."

"Lots of things that happen in this world are crazy. Who would have thought the photographers would have followed us onto that beach?"

"They couldn't have been interested in *me*."

He raised his eyebrows. "Wealthy heiress takes off her shirt for tycoon."

She cringed. "Was that the headline?"

"No, but it could have been." He shook his head. "What I'm saying is these are the cards we've been dealt. We need to do the best we can with this hand." His gaze darkened and he laced his fingers through hers. "In my mind, it could be a winning hand."

Her heart stuttered and she swallowed over a lump in her throat. "How can you feel that way? My father is practically forcing you to marry me."

"No, he's not. I told you before that I'm not a man to be forced into anything by anyone. Especially marriage." He lifted one of his hands to her jaw. "We have something between us. Yeah, the sexual chemistry is outrageous. But there's something else. I like how I feel when I'm with you. I like who I am when I'm with you."

"You're serious," she said, searching his gaze. "But don't you feel trapped? That's what I couldn't bear. The idea of trapping you."

"Before you walked in that door today, I knew we needed to get married."

"But it's so archaic," she said, fear and hope warring inside her.

"It's not archaic," he said. "It's right. Tell me that deep down there isn't something inside you that feels good about this idea. You feel good about being with me all the time, about having me as your husband. Down the line, having babies together," he said, putting his hand on her belly.

Mallory's breath froze somewhere between her lungs and her throat. "I always thought you were trying to avoid marriage. Why would you be willing to make a commitment now?"

"I told you. Because it's the right thing to do. You know it, too."

Mallory closed her eyes. Her head was spinning. Alex wasn't professing undying love. In fact, he hadn't mentioned love at all. She felt a twist of longing inside her. This wasn't what she'd pictured for her marriage.

She forced her eyes open. "What if this is a disaster?"

He gave a rough chuckle and pulled her into his arms. "Mallory, in our own way, you and I are over-achievers. There's no way this will be a disaster."

She buried her head in his shoulder. "I just wish things could be different."

"They will be," he said. "After we're married."

Just like that, the decision was made and wedding plans were put into motion. Exhibiting more enthusiasm than she had in years, her mother plunged into making the arrangements. Her father insisted the wedding take place in ten days.

Alex presented her with a ring that felt strange on her finger. Mallory enlisted Lilli's assistance to help her find a dress.

Standing in front of a three-way mirror after she'd tried on six dresses, Mallory shook her head. "I look like I'm wearing meringue. None of these seem right," she said.

Lilli chuckled, adjusting the gown slightly. "Are you sure it's the dresses?" she asked gently. "Or is it the man?"

"I can't think about that," Mallory said, returning to the dressing room. She hadn't told Lilli about the scandalous photographs of her and Alex. It was too humiliating. "Just trust me, when I tell you that Alex and I have our reasons for getting married."

"But so quickly," Lilli said, following her. "Why can't you take your time?"

"There's a good reason," she said, pushing the gown down and stepping out of it.

Lilli shook it out and returned the garment to the hanger. Then she turned to Mallory. "Are you pregnant?" she asked in a quiet voice.

"No," Mallory instantly replied. "Pregnancy would be easier than—" She broke off and shook her head.

Lilli gave her a blank stare. "I'm dying of curiosity, but if you don't want to tell me, I won't force it."

Mallory sighed and closed her eyes. "It's just so embarrassing. When Alex and I took our trip together, we visited a private beach and…" She opened her eyes and waved her hand.

Lilli's eyes widened. "Oh." She paused. "But I still don't see why you would need to rush into marriage."

"Because someone took pictures of us," Mallory whispered, misery and shame rushing through her again.

"Oh, no," Lilli said, putting her arm around Mallory's shoulder in sympathy.

"They've shown up on the Internet on an obscure site, but it's just a matter of time before someone figures out who the couple in the photos are. My father wants Alex and I married before the story really comes out so it will seem like old news."

Lilli nodded. "And what do you want?"

Mallory shook her head. "I don't know. Alex and

I had begun to connect in a way I'd never thought possible, and I mean more than sexually. But we weren't ready for this."

"He'd asked you to move in with him," Lilli pointed out.

"Yes, but—" Mallory broke off, feeling a sharp twist in her stomach. "He hasn't said he loves me," she admitted.

"Have you told him that you love him?" Lilli asked.

"No," Mallory said and fiddled with the elaborate skirt of the slip. "It seemed too soon."

"I can tell you from personal experience that just because a couple doesn't say I love you before the wedding doesn't mean they will never say it," she said with a soft smile. "It also doesn't mean their marriage can't become a dream come true."

Mallory looked into Lilli's clear blue eyes and found a drop of hope that soothed some of her doubts. "How can we make this work?"

Lilli smiled again. "Just take it one step at a time."

A knock sounded on the dressing room door. "Hello, ladies," the bridal consultant said. "I have some more dresses for you to try."

Mallory met Lilli's gaze and gave a wry smile. "Step one, find a dress I can live with."

Eight

"This was supposed to be simple and small," Mallory said to her father, gaping at the number of people packed into the chapel as she peeked from a tiny window. "How many people are in there?"

Her father patted her hand. "I don't know. Your mother said the guest list kept growing. I haven't seen her this excited about anything in a long, long time," he said.

Mallory met his gaze. "Since Wynn died," she said, feeling a tug of sadness.

Her father nodded. "I know it's been difficult for you to become our only child. We probably didn't handle everything the way we should. And your mother's depression—" He broke off as if he were overcome with emotion.

Mallory was caught off guard by the display. "You two have been wonderful parents."

Her father smiled. "You're so sweet. You sure as hell didn't get that from me." He inhaled deeply. "I just want you to know that I've always been proud of you, and you are a beautiful bride. Megalos is a lucky man."

Her heart twisted with emotions she hadn't expected to feel. She'd been in such a rush to prepare herself for today that she hadn't had much time to think about her parents' feelings. Her eyes swelled with tears. "I love you, Daddy. I hope you'll always be proud of me."

"Always," he said and kissed her cheek. He pulled back and stood taller. "It's time."

She nodded, her stomach fluttering like a hummingbird's wings. Her father gave a soft tap on the door and it immediately opened. At the sight of everyone in that chapel turning to look at her, then standing, her throat tightened with anxiety. She bit the inside of her lip to keep it from quivering.

Then she looked ahead and saw Alex. Gorgeous Alex with so many more layers than she'd dreamed. Wearing a classic black tux, he stood with his feet slightly apart, his hands folded in front of him. With his gaze fixed on hers, she felt as if she was the only other person in the room.

His lips lifted just a bit, giving a hint of his pleasure at seeing her as she walked down the aisle. She smiled and gave her mother a tiny wave just before she arrived at the front of the chapel. Her mother smiled broadly in response.

She finished the last few steps and looked at Alex as he joined her and her father in front of the chaplain. Her heart turned over like a whirling tumbleweed.

"Dearly beloved," she heard the minister say, but her awareness of Alex squeezed everything else from her mind. She was only aware of him, his height, his strength, his incredible magnetism. Was she really going to be his wife?

"Her mother and I," her father said in reply to something the chaplain had asked. Mallory blinked as her father kissed her cheek and joined her hand with Alex's.

His hand felt strong wrapped around hers. Today, more than ever, she needed that strength. She wondered if he suffered from doubts. Surely he did. This had been as much a surprise to him as it had been to her.

Seconds passed and Alex turned her toward him. She stared into his handsome face and wanted to know his heart. She wanted to be in his heart.

His eyes burned into hers. In his green gaze, she saw encouragement, support, strength and…possibilities. Oh, how she wanted those possibilities to come true for both of them.

"Do you, Alex, take Mallory to be your wife? To have and to hold…"

"I do," Alex said, and she felt the click of a lock. She knew he was tying himself to her and her to him. Heaven help them both.

The reception was held in an exquisite private ballroom with marble floors, gold mirrors and crystal chandeliers. Her parents had spared no expense. The menu was sumptuous and the room dripped with white roses on every available surface from the tables to the piano.

She thanked another couple for coming and felt her cheeks ache from smiling. All the tension of the previous ten days was catching up to her and more than anything, she craved a quiet corner. But there was still the first dance and the cake to cut.

Alex dipped his mouth to her ear. "How are you doing?"

She smiled at his timing. It was as if he'd known her energy was starting to flag. "How much longer do we have to stay?" she whispered.

He chuckled. "As far as I'm concerned, we can leave now."

Severely tempted, she shook her head. "We need to do some of the traditional things for the sake of—" She shrugged. "Of whoever cares. We should dance."

"That I don't mind," he said and led her to the dance floor. He spoke with the band for a second and then took her in his arms. The strains of the song that had been playing on the beach began. An old song that had been remade again and again, the tune and words made her smile.

"Up On The Roof," she said, her heart twisting at the romantic selection. "Nice choice."

"I thought so since we'll be spending a lot of evenings on the roof of my penthouse." He spun her around and she laughed. "That's the first real smile I've seen on your face today."

She nodded and closed her eyes so she could seal this moment in her mind. Opening her eyes, she met his gaze, full of hope and wishes. She wondered if he could see them written on her face. She wondered if he felt the same way.

The first dance of their married life together and Mallory whirled from Alex's arms to her father's to partner after partner. The wedding planner finally rescued her, pulling her aside for the cake-cutting.

"It's that time," the woman said in a cheerful voice. "Now if we could just find your groom."

Mallory looked around the room, unable to find Alex. "I don't see—" She double tracked over a corner where a tall blond woman and Alex appeared to be engaged in an intense conversation. The woman lifted her hand to his cheek and Mallory felt as she'd been stabbed. She looked away. "I'm sure he'll be here soon. I would love a sip of water, please," she said.

"Let me get that for you," the woman said. "Can't have our bride getting parched."

Mallory bit her lip, wondering who the woman was. She looked familiar, but she couldn't quite place her. A guest approached her and she plastered on a smile.

Minutes later, the wedding planner returned with Alex, who wore an inscrutable expression. She felt him studying her face, but couldn't bear to look him in the eye.

"I think we need to call it a night," Alex said to the wedding planner. "Mallory is tired."

The wedding planner pressed the bottle of water into her hand. "Just a little longer, I promise. Cut the cake and ten minutes of pleasantries, then out the door."

"Five minutes," Alex said in a firm voice. "My wife is tired."

The wedding planner raised her eyebrows in surprise, but nodded. "This way, then."

Alex led Mallory to the table and she still couldn't look at him. "What's wrong?" he asked in a low voice.

"I could ask you the same," she said and accepted the knife. Alex placed his hand over hers and they cut the first piece. Cameras flashed.

Alex lifted a bite to her lips and Mallory wondered if she would be able to swallow even that small bite. She took it into her mouth and forced it down her dry throat then offered his bite to him.

He surprised her, capturing her hand and kissing

it after he swallowed his bite. The wedding guests roared in approval.

Mallory was filled with confusion. A champagne glass was placed in her hand and she looped her hand through Alex's. Forced to look at him, she saw the possessiveness in his gaze and felt her stomach drop to her knees. What had she let herself in for?

Alex took her glass and his, placed them on the table then pulled her into his arms. She stiffened.

"It's almost over," he promised and covered her mouth with his, surprising her again with his passion. When he pulled away, she was trembling.

Alex lifted his hand to the applauding crowd. "Thank you for coming. Please enjoy the rest of the party. Good night," he said and guests tossed rose petals as he led her out of the room.

Alex had arranged for them to stay in the resort's penthouse suite for the night. He guided her to the private elevator. As soon as the doors whooshed closed, he turned to her. "What's wrong?"

She leaned her head back against the cool steel wall and closed her eyes. She didn't know whether to cry or scream.

"Mallory, why are you upset?"

She sucked in an indignant breath and met his gaze. "Why in the world would I be upset when you are in the corner with a beautiful blond woman at our wedding reception?"

Realization crossed his face and he sighed,

rubbing his hand over his face. "You weren't supposed to see that."

She blinked. "That makes everything better." The elevator doors opened and she stalked toward the doors decorated in ivy and roses.

"Dammit, wait a minute," he said, catching her arm. "I meant I didn't want you upset. That was Chloe. She crashed the reception. I was trying to avoid a big scene by having security remove her from the room."

Mallory met his gaze. "Really?"

He nodded. "Really."

She took an extra breath. "Do you always have this kind of problem when you break up with a woman?"

"Never like this. I'm starting to see the reason for restraining orders," he said, his gaze troubled.

"Should we do something about this? About her?" Mallory asked.

Alex looked at her for a long moment and lifted his hand to her cheek. "You just gave me an amazing gift."

"What?" she asked, confused.

"You said *we*. Should *we* do something? Even though you're miffed," he said, rubbing his finger over her mouth as if it were a lush flower.

Mallory felt some of the fight drain out of her. "Just imagine if the tables were turned," she said. "If you'd seen me in the corner with another man at our wedding reception."

"That's easy," Alex said. "I would have made a scene and given him a bloody nose. You handled it with much more class." He glanced at the door. "Why are we standing outside?"

With no warning, he picked her up and carried her to the door, pushed it open and brought her inside where the room was lit with oodles of candles and dozens of white roses. "What are you—"

"The threshold tradition," he said. "It's supposed to bring good luck. Everyone can use good luck."

He looked down at her and took her mouth with his in a searing, possessive kiss that left her breathless. "What was that for?"

"Because I've been wanting to kiss you all night," he said, sinking onto a white leather sofa and holding her on his lap.

"You've already kissed me several times today."

"Not like I wanted," he said. "Not enough." He rubbed his lip over hers from side to side in delicious, sensual movements. "You feel so good," he said, sliding his tongue over her bottom lip. "Taste so good."

"It's the cake," she said. "I taste like wedding cake."

He gave a dirty chuckle. "Trust me. It's not the cake," he said and took her mouth in another kiss. After a moment, he pulled back and tugged off her shoes. "Bet you're ready to get rid of these."

She nodded and it began to sink in that she had gotten married. She was now his wife. The notion made her chest tighten with a strange mixture of emotion.

"And your dress," he said with a devil's look in his eyes. "Bet you're ready to get rid of that, too."

She couldn't keep a smile of amusement from her face. "Good luck. This dress has fifty buttons."

He shot her a look of disbelief then glanced at her book. "What idiot thought of that?"

"A very famous designer."

"Who is clearly a man-hater," he said and lifted his hand to the buttons. "Good thing I've got staying power."

She lifted her hand to his shoulder and met his gaze. "Do you?" she asked. "Do you really have staying power?"

He paused, clearly hearing her serious tone. "Yes, I do."

Mallory bit her lip, but felt a resolve strengthen inside her. "I don't want to be married to you if you're going to have other women."

His face turned dead serious. "There will be no other women for me, no other men for you," he said in a low, rough voice.

His latter comment caught her off guard. She would never consider being with another man. Now that she'd been with him, now that she'd been his wife, how could she think of anyone but Alex?

"Do you understand?" he asked, lacing his long fingers with hers.

She nodded. "Of course."

"I take my wedding vows seriously, Mallory. I'm committed to you," he said.

She nodded, but her mind was still full of questions. The biggest was would he ever love her?

"I'm your husband," he said, his hands moving over her buttons, releasing them with a speed that surprised her. "Soon enough, there won't be an inch of you that doesn't know that you are my wife."

They spent the night making love until Mallory was too exhausted to continue. She fell asleep in Alex's strong arms and awakened to his kisses. He made love to her again and they shared a delicious meal before it was time to leave.

Alex's job made it impossible to leave his work for a honeymoon. He swept her off her feet and carried her inside his condo. "Welcome home, Mrs. Megalos," he said and allowed her to slide down his body until her feet touched the floor. "The movers will bring anything you want from your parents' place. Just give instructions to the housekeeper and she'll handle everything. I want you to feel comfortable here, so feel free to convert one of the other bedrooms into an office if you like. I'll leave a charge card for you in the morning. Something's up with the board of directors, so I'll need to go in early."

Her heart twisted at the notion of him leaving, which was silly. Having his undivided attention for the last twenty-four hours had knocked her equilibrium completely off-kilter.

He studied her face as if he could read her mind. "You'll be okay, won't you?"

"Of course," she said, refusing to give into her weakness for him. Alex would need a strong woman for his wife, so she needed to buck up and pull herself together. "I have plenty to do to get settled here and make-up work for my class. We can have dinner tomorrow night on the upper terrace."

"Sounds good," he said. "But it may need to be late. I only got half the story from Max at the reception, but it's sounding like we may be in for a major reorganization. I'll send in the housekeeper to unpack for you while I check my messages and give you a chance to relax."

Two hours later she sat propped up in bed, staring at her laptop screen. Feeling a shadow cross over her, she glanced up to see her husband leaning over her wearing a towel looped around his waist and, she suspected nothing else.

His green eyes full of seduction, he shot a quick glance at the laptop. "Anything you need to save?" he asked.

She nodded tearing her gaze from the sight of his amazing body. She wondered if the time would ever come when he didn't take her breath away. She marked the Web site for future research, saved her notes and turned off her laptop.

He immediately took the laptop from her and set it on the dresser. Dropping his towel seconds before he turned off the bedside lamp, he climbed into bed, covering her body with his.

Mallory shivered in anticipation.

"You're not cold, are you?" he asked, sliding his warm hands under her pajama tank top.

"No."

"Good, because you're wearing entirely too many clothes," he said and pulled her top over her head. His hard chest rubbed deliciously against hers, causing a riot in all her most sensitive places. He took her mouth in a hot kiss and pushed her shorts and panties down her legs.

He immediately found her sweet spot with his talented fingers. After a few strokes, he had her panting. "Open up, sweetheart," he told her and as she slid her thighs apart, he thrust inside her, claiming her again, all the way to her core.

Alex left before she woke the next morning. Their days fell into a pattern where Alex left early, arrived home late, worked a couple hours after dinner, made love to Mallory and fell asleep.

An uneasiness inside her began to grow. Was this going to be their future? A distracted dinner followed by late-night sex? It almost seemed as if they talked less now than they had before they'd married.

She wanted to get through to Alex. She wanted him to see her. She wanted him to, heaven help her, love her. Mallory racked her brain for ways to get to him. She tried to meet him for lunch during the day. She invited him to play golf. He was always apologetic, but always too busy.

One evening when Alex was working late again and Mallory was trying her best not to sulk, the condo phone rang and when she answered it, she knew she'd found a way to get Alex's attention.

"Thursday night's not good for me," Alex said absently to Mallory as he made a mental note to himself about the resort in West Virginia. "I'm working late."

"Not on Thursday night. Change your plans," she said in an airy, but confident voice as she sipped her wine during their late dinner.

Surprised that she would disagree with him, he shook his head. "I can't change them. I have a late meeting with marketing then I have a conference call with three contractors in West Virginia."

"Reschedule," she said, surprising him again with her insistence.

"Sweetheart, you don't understand—"

"No," she corrected. "You don't understand. I need you to be available on Thursday night. I need you to go somewhere with me."

"Mallory, be reasonable."

"I am. Do you know how many evenings you've spent with me since we got married?"

"I told you this month was going to be tough. I have an unusually heavy workload partly due to the construction project in West Virginia. Maybe we could schedule something for Sunday night."

She shook her head stubbornly. "No. It has to be Thursday."

"Tell me what it is," he said.

She took a deep breath. "A surprise."

She was such a tenderhearted woman, he thought. Lord he was lucky he hadn't married one of those sharp, brittle women he'd dated during the last several years. "That's sweet," he said. "But I really can't cancel—"

"You have to," she said. "Or I—I'll have to do something desperate."

Alex blinked at her. "What the hell—"

She rose from the table, her meal nearly untouched. "I mean it. I've made plans. I need your presence on Thursday night, and as your wife, I shouldn't have to—" Her voice broke and she bit her lip. "Beg."

Swearing under his breath, Alex stood and reached for her. "You're feeling neglected. Dammit. I can't change my schedule."

She pulled back and lifted her hands. "Don't try to charm me. Don't use seduction. Do you realize I've seen you for an average of sixty waking minutes each day since we got married? I'm just asking for one night," she said, her voice breaking again. Clearly appalled at herself, she spun around and ran from the dining room to the terrace, whisking the door closed behind her.

Alex swore under his breath and rubbed a hand

over his face. The downside of marrying a woman with heart was dealing with her sensitivities. Alex's primary focus was his career. His role at Megalos-De Luca Enterprises was his destiny. Everything else came second. Relationships, his needs, his desires. Everything. Now that he was forging ahead on his individual resort project, more was demanded from him than ever.

As his wife, she would need to grow accustomed to his schedule. His first mistress was his work. This once, however, he would bend, but he would make it clear that in the future, she should never make plans that required his presence without consulting him first.

Thursday night arrived and Alex's chauffeur drove Alex and Mallory to the address she'd given him. Mallory was scared spitless. Her palms were clammy, her heart raced. Her only saving grace was that Alex was distracted by a call he'd received on his cell phone. For once, she was thankful for the interruption.

The more she thought about it, the more she feared this may not have been such a good idea after all. Alex might not appreciate his new wife interfering. By the end of the evening, he could very well be furious with her.

Her stomach twisted into another knot and she tried to rein in her fear. Her instincts had screamed that this was the right thing for her to do. She prayed she was right.

Todd pulled in front of the entrance to the lecture hall and he opened the door for Alex and Mallory to exit the Bentley. Alex wrapped up his call and curiously glanced at the building. "Thanks, Todd," Alex said then turned to Mallory as he escorted her inside. "Are you going to tell me what this is all about now?"

"No," she said, forcing a smile to her face as they approached an auditorium. "You'll know soon enough."

Alex gave a long-suffering sigh. "Do we have assigned seats?"

"Yes," she said, her stomach twisting and turning. "Near the front."

They took their seats and Mallory held her breath.

"You're really not going to tell me," Alex murmured in her ear.

"I'm really not," she said and prayed this would all turn out right.

Finally the lights dimmed and a gray-haired man mounted the platform. "Ladies and gentleman, as director of bio-genetic studies for the University of Nevada, it is my honor and pleasure to introduce this evening's speaker, Dr. Gustavas Megalos…"

Mallory slid a sideways glance at Alex as his brother's name was announced. His eyes rounded in surprise and his gaze was fixed on the podium as a man with dark hair and glasses climbed the platform.

"Gus," he whispered, leaning toward her. "How the hell did you know he was coming to town?"

"He called and said he wanted to see you," she said, trying unsuccessfully to read her husband.

"You couldn't just tell me," he said.

"I didn't know how you would respond. It was too important to risk you saying no."

His jaw tightened. "That's why you said you would do something desperate."

She swallowed over the knot in her throat. "Yes. Are you angry?"

"I'm surprised," he said and focused on his brother.

Mallory suffered in limbo as Alex's brother discussed the importance of genetic studies and the advancements that had been made. She stole glances at Alex throughout the lecture, trying to read him, but his expression was inscrutable.

She hoped she'd made the right decision. That time Alex had opened up to her, she'd glimpsed a longing for his family. She prayed this would be a turning point, and that Alex could reconnect with his family.

Alex's brother finished his speech and the crowd applauded. Alex turned to Mallory. "You want to tell me the rest of the plan now?"

"There's a bar next door. You and your brother can go there and have a beer together," she said, feeling a spark of hope.

"What about you?" Alex asked.

"I'll go home."

Alex shook his head. "I want my brother to meet my wife," he said, standing and extending his hand to her.

Her heart dipped at his words and the emotions she read in his eyes. Maybe, she felt herself begin to hope more and more, maybe Alex could grow to love her after all.

Nine

One week later, Mallory and Alex attended a charity gala held at the Grand Trillion Resort and Casino. After Alex's successful visit with his brother, Mallory's confidence had begun to climb. Although Alex still worked late, he'd begun to call her during the day, and if she wasn't mistaken, she was seeing a new light in his eyes when he looked at her. As for her own feelings, she felt as if she was glowing from the inside out. Her heart was traveling in uncharted waters with him. She'd never felt so strongly about a man, but now she had reason to hope their marriage would work.

Unable to keep a smile from her face, she glanced

around the room and saw her father wave. She and Alex visited him at the bar.

Mallory kissed her father on the cheek. "Hi, Daddy. How's business? Ready to hire me?"

Her father choked on his whiskey, pounding his chest. He scowled at her. "You shouldn't frighten an old man like that when he's got half a glass of whiskey in his throat."

"I'm not that scary," she said.

"No, but you don't need a job," he told her giving her a quick squeeze. "You have a husband to take care of you now."

Getting married hadn't changed Mallory's desire to prove herself professionally, but she could see that it would be futile to argue with her father. "Where's Mom?" she asked, looking around the beautiful room.

"She's over there talking to one of our neighbors. I have to tell you, Mallory. Your wedding did wonders for her. She's getting out more, taking some kind of exercise class. Plating or something."

"Pilates," Mallory said, trading a smile of amusement with Alex.

"She's trying to get me to go with her," he said, clearly appalled.

"You should try it," she said. "It would be good for you."

He shook his head. "I'll stick to golf. Go give her a kiss. She'll be glad to see you."

Spotting her mother in a cluster of women, Mallory walked toward her. Her mother glanced up and smiled, breaking slightly away from the other women. "Hi, sweetheart. I told your father I was looking forward to seeing you tonight."

"Thanks." Mallory kissed her mother on her cheek. "It's good to see you, too. You look wonderful."

"You look wonderful, too," her mother said. "Something about seeing you get married made an impact on me. Life does go on, doesn't it?" she asked, with a hint of her former fragility in her eyes.

Mallory knew what her mother was saying. She still suffered over Wynn, but after all this time, it seemed she finally saw the need to start living again. "Yes, it does. I know I've told you this before, but thank you for all the work you did for my wedding."

Her mother smiled. "That was my pleasure. You're my only daughter, so that was my only chance. I'm doing pretty well. I've even started exercising."

"That's what Daddy told me. That's great," Mallory said.

"Now if I can just talk him into quitting cigars and Scotch," her mother said.

"Then you'll be performing a miracle," Mallory said.

Her mother laughed. Although it was an odd rusty, unfamiliar sound, Mallory felt a rush of tenderness.

"You may be right," her mother said. "I should let you get back to your handsome, new husband."

Mallory looked over her shoulder at Alex and felt her heart skip over itself. Longing, deep and powerful, twisted through her. As every day passed, she found herself wanting his love more and more. "I'm sure I'll see you again later," she said and kissed her mother once more.

She walked toward her father and Alex. With their backs facing her, she decided to surprise them. As she crept closer, she heard her father talking.

"I told you I would reward the man who could get my daughter happily down the aisle. It may have taken some extra pushing, but you succeeded. Her mother and I are very pleased. Mallory just doesn't understand that she needs a protective influence in her life. You provide that for her."

Mallory frowned at her father's words. *Reward? Happily down the aisle? A protective influence?* Had her father actually offered Alex a reward to marry her? Her stomach twisted with nausea. She stared at the two men in disbelief. It couldn't be true, she thought. It couldn't be.

"She's more adventurous than I originally thought," Alex said. "When you first talked about matchmaking, I thought she would need a much milder, more conservative man than me. After spending some time with her, I wasn't sure any of my friends could keep her busy enough to stay out of trouble."

Mallory gasped, unable to keep the shocked sound

from escaping her throat. Alex must have heard her because he immediately turned around. His gaze met hers and she instantly knew she'd caught him at his game. The terrible secret was out. He'd never really wanted her as his wife. He'd obviously just wanted something from her father, although she couldn't imagine what Alex could need because her so-called husband was plenty wealthy.

"Mallory, don't misunderstand," Alex began.

"I don't think I do," she said, torn between humiliation and devastating pain. She felt like such a fool, and she'd hoped he would eventually love her. He had no intention of loving her. She was just a game piece he'd used to win something obviously more important to him.

He moved toward her and she shook her head, backing away.

"You didn't want to marry me because of any feelings for me," she said, her throat nearly closing shut from the pain.

"Baby, don't overreact," her father said.

She shot him a quelling glance. "And you made it all happen. I was so stupid," she said, hating that her voice broke. "So stupid. I actually thought you wanted me," she said to Alex. A horrible pressure at the back of her eyelids formed, making her feel as if she would burst into tears any second. She refused to give into it.

"I feel like such an idiot. And here I was trying my

best to be a good wife when it was all a sham." Her voice broke again. "I want a divorce," she said and fled the room.

The hurt Alex saw in Mallory's eyes stabbed him like a dagger. He turned to Edwin James. "Are you okay, sir?" he asked.

Edwin's face was pale. "I could be better, but I'll be okay. I'm not as sure about my daughter," he said then grimly met Alex's gaze. "I'm not so sure about you."

"If you're okay, then I need to go talk to my wife," Alex told him.

Edwin lifted his eyebrows. "By all means, do."

Alex immediately clicked into crisis mode and left the ballroom. He ruthlessly pushed back his emotions, putting a plan together and executing it at the same time. Dammit, he wished Mallory hadn't heard that conversation. Lengthening his stride, he headed for the front door, suspecting she would try to get the car or grab a cab. He took the stairs instead of the elevator and rounded two corners before he arrived at the resort entrance. Mallory was stepping into a cab.

He quickly jogged toward the cab and grabbed the door as she began to close it.

Mallory stared up at him. "What are you doing? Go away. Leave me alone. I don't want anything to do with you." She let out a squeak when he wouldn't let her close the door. *"What are you doing!"* she shrieked.

"I'm getting in this cab with *my wife*," he said and slid into the back seat, pushing her over and pulling the door closed behind him.

Mallory immediately darted for the other side of the cab and reached for the door handle. Alex reached across her to hold down the lock. "Drive," he said to the cabdriver.

"Where?" the driver asked with a wary expression on his face.

"Let me go!" Mallory yelled.

"Around," Alex said, absorbing the ineffective blows from Mallory's pelting hands.

The driver glanced at him doubtfully from the rearview mirror. "I'm not sure I should—"

"I'm her husband," Alex said, lifting his head when Mallory aimed her hand at his face. "Please note. She's hitting me, not the other way around."

The cabdriver nodded. "Oh, okay," he said and moved the car forward.

"Damn you," Mallory said. "I have nothing to say to you. The only reason you married me was to get something from my father. I have nothing but disgust for you."

"I didn't marry you just because of your father," he said, determined to remain calm.

"But that was part of the reason."

He shook his head. "As you know, there were several factors. The photos from the beach pushed things along," he said.

"If there even were photos from the beach. I never saw them," she retorted.

"I can show you if you'd like to see them. I was trying to protect you from embarrassment," he said.

"Protection," she echoed vehemently. "Who are you protecting? Yourself or me?"

Alex gritted his teeth. "As I said, I can show you—"

"But the photos weren't really the big deal, were they? The dealmaker for our marriage was my father," she told him, her eyes full of hostility.

"You're upset. You're not thinking clearly," he told her. "There's no way I would have married you if there wasn't something between us, something strong," he said.

"But not love," she said bluntly. "And don't tell me I'm not thinking clearly. This is the first clear thought I've had since I met you. So tell me, did it all work out well for you? Was the deal you made with my father really worth being tied to me? After all, you could have easily been through a dozen women since you met me."

He took her wrist in his hand. "Our marriage wasn't about your father. Have you forgotten that I asked you to move in with me when we were in the islands?"

"You'd already negotiated some kind of deal with my father," she said and looked away, shaking her hand. "I should have known. It was just so easy and you were so attentive. It couldn't have been real."

"It was real," he told her. "Everything you and I did was real. It was between you and me."

"You never took a second look at me until you made your deal with my father," she said, her gaze damning him with the disillusionment he saw there.

"The truth is your father told me you needed a husband and he flat out told me he knew I wasn't the right man for you," he told her.

Her eyes widened in surprise. "What?"

"He asked me if I knew anyone who would be a good match for you. In the beginning, when I first tried to get you to meet with me, it was so I could find out your likes and dislikes and introduce you to some men who might work for you."

Her jaw dropped. "You've got to be kidding."

He shook his head. "Trouble was the more I got to know you, the more men I eliminated from the list. I decided I was the right one for you."

She stared at him for a long moment as if she were trying to digest his explanation. She shook her head. "That's ridiculous. I don't believe it."

"Fine. Ask your father," he said.

"As if he would tell the truth," she said. "He would agree with anything you say."

"*Your father* would agree to *anything?*" he said more than asked.

She met his gaze for a long moment then looked away. "This is still ridiculous. And I'm still getting a divorce. I won't stay in this sham of a marriage."

Despite the fact that Alex was known as a master persuader, a master negotiator, he was rock-solid on some issues. Marriage was one of them. "There will be no divorce," he said quietly.

She looked at him as if he were crazy. "Excuse me? You can't force me to stay with you. It's perfectly reasonable that I wouldn't want to stay in a marriage based on lies."

He gave a harsh laugh. "Every couple who gets married is lying to each other. The woman lies about liking sports. The man lies about liking her family. Marriage is often based on a pack of lies. The deception may be made with good intentions, but it's still deception."

She shook her head, looking at him as if she didn't know him at all. "You're so full of cynicism. No wonder you don't believe in love." She glanced away. "How stupid of me to hope that you and I—" She broke off and stared out the window. "I still want a divorce."

"I've already said that's not an option. A Megalos never divorces," he said.

"Interesting time for you to pull out the family card given the fact that you don't even speak to your family anymore," she said.

He withstood the low blow. "That wasn't like you, Mallory."

He watched her take a deep breath. "Perhaps not," she said. "This situation isn't bringing out the best in me. *You* aren't bringing out the best in me. The wisest thing to do is for us to quietly divorce and get on with our lives. It would take very little time to—"

"I told you we're not getting a divorce. I'll fight you every inch of the way."

"Why?" she demanded, turning around, full of fire and fury. "I could name a dozen reasons why we shouldn't stay together."

"We've made a commitment," he said. "We've taken vows. Those are the reasons we'll stay together."

"But those vows have nothing to do with love, past, present or future. You don't even really believe in love. Why be miserable?"

"Misery isn't necessary. Just because you're facing reality instead of relying on romantic wishful thinking doesn't mean we can't be happy. We can work it out and reach a deal to make a happy life for ourselves," he said.

She made a face. "You make it sound like a business negotiation."

"Ask you father. Ask your friend. Ask anyone who's been married. Marriage is one negotiation after another."

"And the reason you married me is because you thought you could win them all because I was so easy," she said, full of resentment. "I need to be away from you. I need some space." She turned to the cabdriver. "Drop me off at the Bellagio, please."

"No. Take us here instead," he said and gave the

address for his house on the outskirts of town. He wanted privacy.

"I'm not staying with you," Mallory said. "I can't. And you can't make me. I can't bear to be with you one more night."

The change from her adoring, loving attitude cut him to the quick, but he didn't give into it. "There are plenty of bedrooms in my home. Choose one. We can discuss this in the morning."

As soon as Alex opened the door to his home, Mallory flew past him hardly noticing the beautiful decor. She was so upset she barely took in the sight of lush, intricately designed carpets, antique wooden furniture and the sparkle of crystal and mirrors.

"Would you like something to drink?" he asked from behind her.

She quivered at the intimate sound of his voice and despised herself for her reaction to him. She refused to look at him. "While I'm tempted to ask for the biggest bottle of wine you have, I'll just take water," she said. "Can you please point me in the direction of your kitchen?"

"It's down the hall to the left, but all the bedrooms have small refrigerators and bottled water," he said.

She nodded. "Thank you. Now, if you could point me in the direction of the master bedroom?"

His eyebrows lifted in surprise. "Upstairs, far left."

She nodded. "I'll be sleeping at the other end of the house. Good night," she said and felt his gaze taking in her every step. Taking a sharp right at the top of the stairs, she walked all the way to the end and opened the door to a guest room decorated in shades of restful green.

She might have appreciated it more if she weren't so upset. After some searching, she found the mini-fridge discreetly hidden in a cabinet. She pulled out a bottle of water and took several swallows as she paced the carpet.

Mallory rubbed her forehead. How had she gotten herself into this situation? Her father had deceived her. Alex had deceived her. A bitter taste filled her mouth. Perhaps she had even deceived herself.

Sure, in the beginning, she had kept her guard up around Alex. She'd continually reminded herself that he was a player and she would never hold his interest. The more time she'd spent with him, though, the more she'd wanted to believe he was sincere. *What a fool.*

A knock sounded on the door. Alex, she thought and scowled. "Go away."

A brief silence followed. "Mr. Megalos asked me to bring you some things for your stay," said a timid female voice.

Cringing at her rudeness, Mallory rushed to the door. "I'll just leave them—"

Mallory opened the door to a woman dressed in a black uniform with a hesitant expression on her face. The woman held a large basket that contained toiletries and a robe.

"I'm so sorry. I thought you were—" Mallory broke off. "Someone else. Thank you. This is lovely."

"You're very welcome," the woman said, smiling cautiously. "I'm Gloria, and may I congratulate you on your recent marriage to Mr. Megalos."

Please don't, Mallory wanted to say, but swallowed the urge. "Thank you."

"May I get anything else for you?" Gloria asked. "A snack?"

Mallory's stomach was still upset. She didn't know when she would want to eat again. "No, thank you. This will be fine. Thank you again, and good night," she said and closed the door. Waiting a few seconds for Gloria to walk away, Mallory locked the door. She didn't want a surprise intruder, particularly one that stood six feet tall and was entirely too handsome and charming.

She couldn't believe the two most important men in her life could have done such a thing to her. Did her father truly believe she was incapable of making good decisions for herself?

Her stomach twisted into another knot.

She felt so betrayed. She would do anything to escape to somewhere far, far away from both Alex and her father. Europe, she fantasized, or Australia.

Not likely. Mallory frowned. Both Alex and her father would have their goons watching her every move.

Sinking onto the bed, she crossed her arms over her chest. Everything inside her ached. It was a wrenching sensation as if she were being ripped apart. Even though she and Alex had only been married for a month, she'd become his wife in her mind, and heaven help her in her heart and soul.

And it had all been a trick.

Remnants of the first overwhelming rush of anger still lingered, but other unwanted emotions trickled through her fury. Bone-deep sadness and gaping loss the size of a black hole sucked her downward.

Her chest and throat tightened like a vise closing around her. She felt so lost. A sob escaped her throat, then another. She'd been determined not to cry in front of Alex, but it was as if a dam broke and unleashed her tears.

Stripping off her clothes, she crawled into bed and cried herself to sleep.

A sliver of dawn crept through the window the next morning, waking Mallory. She lay in bed in a semisleep state, wondering if Alex was already up and drinking his coffee. He rose earlier than anyone she knew, even her father.

Her eyes still closed, she sniffed the air for the

scent of coffee, but the only thing she smelled was the unfamiliar scent of lavender. She frowned to herself.

Any minute he would walk back in the room and look at her. She would pretend to be asleep for a maximum of thirty excruciating seconds, then she would open her eyes and smile, and he would lean over her and kiss her good-morning....

Mallory sighed, waiting for the sound of his footsteps. She heard nothing and forced her eyes open even though they felt weighted down with concrete blocks.

Everything that had happened last night hit her at once. Emotions jabbed at her ruthlessly. Humiliation. Loss. Anger.

She pulled the sheet over her head to hide. Oh, heaven help her, what was she going to do now?

She'd seen the expression on his face. He wouldn't let her go. Alex possessed the personality of a conqueror, and he knew far more about winning than she did. Any chance of her resistance was doomed.

She burrowed deeper under the covers. All she wanted to do was hide. How long, some rational part of her mind asked. How many years would she hide?

The same way her mother had.

Mallory immediately tossed back the sheet and sat up in one swift motion. "Damn it," she said. "Damn him."

Alex may have destroyed one of the deepest wishes in her heart, but she had other goals, other dreams. Mallory refused to stop living.

Ten

"**I** want a job," Mallory said, her hands folded in her lap, her gaze steadfast. Her glorious wavy hair was pulled back into a ponytail at her nape and she emanated as much warmth as an icicle.

Alex could hardly believe the change from his sweet, adoring and passionate bride to the cool, remote woman sitting on the chair opposite him.

"A job," he echoed, rolling the word around his mouth as he stood.

"That's right. If you insist on us remaining together, then the least you owe me is the opportunity to pursue some of my dreams." She paused a half-beat and her eyes flickered with deep sadness.

"Since some of my dreams will never come true, helping me get a job is the least you can do."

Alex stuffed his hands into his pockets in frustration. "Why do you want to work? You can lead a life of leisure. Or at the least, you can set your own schedule. That's the dream of most American women *and* men."

"This isn't a new goal for me. I mentioned it to you some time ago. If you're deadset against it, you better tell me now. This is a deal breaker," she said in a crisp voice.

Alex was stunned at her inflexibility. He didn't want his wife working. He didn't want his wife to feel it was necessary to work. "You're making this difficult."

"In the grand scheme of things, I'm not asking for all that much."

Resting his hands on his hips, he looked down at her, wondering where the sweet woman who'd been his wife had gone. "I can provide for you. You don't need to work."

"Yes, I do. I *need* to feel as if I'm accomplishing something. I don't want to feel like I'm under someone's thumb." She took a quick breath.

"A job," he said again. Alex hadn't spent much time thinking about his future wife, but he'd always expected his wife to retire from her job once they married. After all, he could provide everything a woman could wish for.

He looked into Mallory's eyes and saw the combination of hurt and determination. The hurt made him feel restless. Resting his hands on his hips, he considered options.

"I'll have to think about it. It's not as if any job would do since you're my wife," he said.

"I'll give you two weeks," she said, coolly meeting his gaze.

He lifted an eyebrow. "Or what?" he asked, surprised again that she would have the nerve to give him a deadline. Daddy's little girl was pushing back.

"Or I walk," she said, rising from her seat. "You may not agree to a divorce, but I don't have to agree to live with you, either."

Even though Alex knew he would eventually win any arguments she presented about living apart, he couldn't help feeling a shocking illicit thrill at the challenge in her eyes, her voice, her body. She oozed a dare to him.

"Fine," he said. "I'll find a position for you. You'll be reviewed by someone other than me. If you don't cut it, then it's back to charity work and being my wife."

She glowered at him. "I can cut anything you throw at me. And as far as being your wife, this has become a business arrangement. It was from the beginning. I just didn't know it. If we're going to have a loveless marriage, it's going to be a sexless marriage."

Alex blinked. She couldn't be serious, not with the chemistry they shared. He laughed. "Good joke."

"I am not joking," she said, looking so furious he

wondered if steam would come pouring out of her ears any minute. "Why should I continue to humiliate myself—"

"I didn't know you found sex with me humiliating," he cut in. "I could have sworn those were sounds of pleasure you were making."

She inhaled sharply. "This marriage is a sham. Everything between us is a sham."

"That's not true and you know it. You're exaggerating because you're still upset," he said and shook his head when she opened her mouth. "This argument is unnecessary. You can stay in another bedroom if that's what you want, but it won't last. Now, is that all?"

She silently met his gaze for a long moment, her hands knotted in fury, her cheeks pink from barely restrained temper. She looked like she wanted to slap him. "Yes," she hissed.

"Then I need to get to work. You can either ride with me or I'll send a driver for you."

"I'm not riding with you," she said. "In fact, I think I'll stay here for the next two weeks."

Alex shook his head. "No. I said you may choose another bedroom, not another house. Besides, we have appearances scheduled for this weekend."

"You can't really expect me to appear with you in public and act as if everything between us is all lovey-dovey."

"I can and I do," he said. "I'll leave you with

something to think about. We didn't profess our love to each other before we were married, and you had no aversion to sharing my bed then. I'll see you tonight at dinner." He leaned toward her to kiss her goodbye, but she turned her head.

Even though Alex had won the argument, the victory was hollow. He hadn't realized how much the affection in Mallory's gaze had felt like a ray of sunshine.

Malloy rode to the condo in a sedan driven by Todd. Scowling at the sunny day, she pumped her foot as she crossed one leg over the other. What she wouldn't give to wring Alex's neck and wipe that insufferable confidence off his face.

She'd never felt more trapped in her life. She felt as if the very life was being choked out of her. How could he possibly expect her to pretend their marriage wasn't just a big show? How could she possibly act as if she adored him when she was already fantasizing about fixing a dinner that would cause him a week's worth of indigestion?

After a while, she would wear him down. He would tire of having a wife in name only. He may not love her, but he wanted her to warm his bed. She scowled again at the thought. She'd been so easy, so eager to please. Now Alex would see a different side of her. A side that would make him give her the freedom she deserved.

Mallory allowed herself to stew over the situation

until she arrived at the condo. Then she chose her new bedroom, the one farthest away from Alex's. No need to tempt him. She wouldn't need to worry about being tempted by him. Now that she knew the truth about him, she couldn't possibly feel even a spark of lust, let alone love. She moved all her clothes and belongings to the room and studied how she could make her new bedroom a place of comfort and solace.

She decided to go shopping for candles, pillows and anything else that caught her attention. At the mall, the local animal league was holding a fund and adoption drive. Mallory stroked the soft fur of the dogs and cats. She'd always wanted a pet, but her mother had been allergic.

But she no longer lived in the same house as her mother. An idea occurred to her as she petted a kitten. If she was looking for comfort, a pet would be perfect. She wondered how Alex would feel about having a pet. It would be inconsiderate to get one without asking his opinion.

On the other hand, it had been incredibly inconsiderate for him to marry her for business reasons, too. Mallory smiled to herself as she looked at the animals. Alex would probably hate having a pet. All the more reason for her to get one, although Mallory would never adopt an animal out of spite. Adopting a pet would be one little dream of hers that she could still make come true. If she and Alex remained married, there would be no children. The realization saddened her. She would need to give her affection to some other living being.

Mallory spent the rest of the afternoon shopping for her new bedroom and the two cats she adopted from the animal shelter. New collars, cat food, an electronic litter box, cat carriers.

As she pulled up to the entrance of the condo, the valet opened the door for her and glanced in her back seat. "Would you like some help taking your bags upstairs?"

"Yes, please. That would be wonderful," Mallory said, grabbing the two cat carriers while her new furry friends made plaintive cries. "I don't think they like the carriers, but I don't trust them loose yet."

The nice valet helped her carry everything up to the penthouse.

As she opened the door, she caught the scent of dinner cooking. Surprised because she hadn't requested anything, she wondered if Alex had called from work with instructions. The prospect of seeing him again almost destroyed her good mood, but when she looked at her new kitties again, she had to smile.

Jean, the housekeeper, walked into the foyer and blinked at the sight of the cat carriers. "Cats?" she said in disbelief.

"Yes, aren't they darling?" Mallory asked. "I'll put them in my room for now, but later—"

"Your room," Jean echoed, grabbing several bags

the valet had deposited at the front door and trying to keep up with Mallory.

"Yes," Mallory said, walking through the den and down the long hallway to the end. "I guess Alex didn't have a chance to tell you, but this will be my room. I may redecorate, but I'll figure that out later." She bent down to let out the long-haired black cat with glowing green eyes. "His name is Gorgeous," she said as she stroked his silky, soft fur.

The other cat mewed in envy and Mallory laughed. "I know. It's your turn, Indie," she said, releasing the short-haired calico and rubbing her under her chin. "Aren't they sweet?"

The housekeeper shot a wary eye at Gorgeous, who'd sprang onto an upholstered chair. She cleared her throat. "Mrs. Megalos, I'm not sure Mr. Megalos is a cat lover."

"That's okay. I'll take care of them," Mallory said.

Jean cleared her throat again then nodded. "Mr. Megalos asked me to tell you as soon as you arrived that the two of you are having dinner on the upper terrace. He asked the chef to prepare your favorite dish."

I'm sure he did, Mallory thought as she narrowed her eyes. If Alex thought Crab Imperial on the terrace was going to be enough to win her back to his bed, then he was sadly mistaken. "Thanks. How soon will it be ready?" Mallory asked.

"He requested that you join him as soon as you arrive," Jean said.

Mallory nodded. "Please tell him I'll be upstairs as soon as I set up the litter box and wash up."

"You want me to mention the litter box?" Jean asked in a strained voice, clearly reluctant to be the bearer of that news.

"Good thinking," Mallory said. "Ask him to come in here so I can surprise him."

The housekeeper looked at her as if she'd lost her mind, but nodded. "As you wish."

As Indie circled around her, Mallory pulled out the litter box and poured the litter into it.

"What the hell—"

Mallory glanced up to find Alex staring at Indie. He met her gaze and even though the real reason she'd gotten the cats was for her own edification, she got a tiny thrill at the look of shock on his face. "A cat?"

"Two," she said with a smile that was completely sincere. She pointed at Gorgeous sitting in the chair. "The volunteers at the animal rescue league told me cats are happier in pairs. I was going to get kittens, but I decided on adults because not as many people want them. Meet Gorgeous and Indie," she said and picked up the calico. "I love cats. Don't you?"

He opened his mouth then rubbed his hand over it. "Tell me again why you got two," he said.

"So they won't be lonely while I'm at work," she said.

Alex clenched his jaw and gave a short nod.

"Dinner's ready. I asked the chef to prepare your favorite."

"Yes, thank you. Jean told me. I'll wash up and join you," she said, feeling the strain between them pull like an overstretched rubber band. She hated the sensation.

Leaving her new furry friends in her new room, she freshened up and climbed the stairs to the upper level of the terrace. A light breeze softened the blazing heat. Alex stood, looking over the balcony, his mind seemingly a million miles away. The wind ruffled his wavy hair and his white shirt. He appeared so isolated. She wondered if he would ever admit to feeling lonely. She wondered if he would ever admit to needing someone. Needing her?

Slamming the door on such useless thoughts, she lifted her chin. She could and would get through this. "The Crab Imperial smells delicious," she said, taking a seat at the table.

Alex glanced up and walked to the table. It struck her that he moved with the grace of a primitive, wild animal. A tiger, she decided. He moved his chair next to hers and sat down, his leg immediately brushing hers.

Mallory's heart skipped and she moved her leg away from his. She wished she wasn't so aware of him. She shouldn't be, she thought, taking a sip of white wine. Not after what he'd done.

"You've been busy today," he said, picking up his fork and taking a bite.

"I had a lot to do," she said and took a bite of the Crab Imperial. It tasted like sawdust.

"You didn't need to move into another room so quickly," he said. "You could have slept on your decision."

"No, I couldn't," she said, suspecting that if she'd slept on her decision she would have never moved out. She would have simply remained under Alex's spell forever, feeling and acting like a weak fool.

She took another bite and it tasted the same, sawdust. Blast it. "What did you find out about jobs for me today?"

He took a long sip of wine and speared a piece of crab with his fork. "Technically nothing."

Mallory's blood pressure immediately rose. "I really meant it when I said I wanted a job. I can interview for one on my own."

"That won't be necessary. I've decided you'll work for me," he said.

She blinked. "How?"

"I've been working double time because of the resort I'm developing in West Virginia. Your father has supplied the investors."

"In trade for you being my husband," she said, a bitter taste filling her mouth.

"He would have done it, anyway. It's a good investment."

"Why was it necessary? You have enough money on your own," she blurted out.

"One of the rules of wealth management is that you use other people's money to accomplish your goals. You don't risk your own."

She was surprised at his acumen, but shouldn't have been. "Where do I fit in with this?"

"I want you to interface with my contacts in West Virginia. There will be very limited travel," he said. "I don't want my wife spending most of her time away from me. I'm balancing several demands at Megalos-De Luca Enterprises and the personal resort start-up, so I won't be able to get your job in place for another week or so."

"As long as it's within two weeks," she said, feeling as if she had to hold the line. Alex had made her forget everything but him. She couldn't let that happen again.

"I'll make it worth the wait," he said in such a sexy way that it sent a shiver down her all the way to her toes.

Upset by her reaction to him, Mallory rushed down a couple of bites of the dish and gulped some wine. "That was delicious. I'm full. If you don't mind excusing me—"

"Already?" he said with a raised eyebrow that could have made her back down in other circumstances. But not now.

"The cats," she said. "I need to get them acclimated to their new home."

He gave a slow nod that made her feel as if she

may have won round one, but the game was far from over. "We have a cocktail party with the other VPs, CEO and board members of Megalos-De Luca Enterprises the day after tomorrow."

She blinked in surprise. "That's not much notice."

"No, it isn't," he said. "The board is introducing a reengineering specialist."

"You don't sound happy," she said.

"I'm not. Neither is Max De Luca."

She shivered at the cold expression on his face. "I can't imagine anyone in their right mind who would want to go up against the two of you."

He lifted his mouth in a smile that bared his teeth like a wolf. "I always thought you were a clever woman."

She stood. "Just not clever enough to see through the ruse you and my father cooked up."

Alex shot from his chair and snagged her wrist. "There was always something between us, Mallory. You can't deny that."

She knew she'd always had feelings for him. That was all. She shook her head. "I have no idea what your true feelings, if any, are for me."

"I can show you," he offered and lowered his head.

She turned her head away and his mouth seared her cheek. Her heart was hammering a mile a minute. "I want more than a man who's interested in me for the money my father can find for him. I want more than sex."

Eleven

The tension at the Megalos-De Luca cocktail party
was so thick it reminded Mallory of trying to breathe
in a dust storm. The room vibrated with such suspi-
cion she couldn't wait to leave.

Spotting Lilli De Luca, she felt a smidgeon of relief
and waved. Lilli smiled in return and moved toward
Mallory. "Hi," she said, giving Mallory a quick hug.
"This is horrible, isn't it?" she said in a low voice.

Mallory gave a short laugh, nodding in agreement. "I couldn't agree more. It feels like we're
waiting for the gallows."

Lilli's pretty features wrinkled in concern. "I
know. Max has been very upset about this. He won't

talk about it, but he's not sleeping well at all. What about Alex?"

Mallory felt a twist of self-consciousness. She didn't know how Alex was sleeping because she wasn't sharing his bed. "He's bothered, too."

Lilli nodded. "The two of them are talking more and more. It's interesting how something like this can turn two men who were competitors into more of a team. You find out a lot about a man by how he acts when the pressure's on."

The discussion made Mallory even more uncomfortable. She would examine why later. "How's David?"

Lilli lit up. She lifted her hand and showed a miniscule of space between her thumb and forefinger. "He's this close to crawling. Max is egging him on even though I keep telling Max we'll both be doing a lot more chasing once David is mobile."

Mallory felt a stab of loss as she thought about the babies she wouldn't have with Alex.

"I'm sure you're still enjoying your honeymoon period," Lilli said with a knowing smile. "What's new at the Megalos house?"

"Cats," Mallory said. "I adopted two cats."

Lilli gaped. "Oh, my gosh. How did Alex react to that?"

"Surprisingly well," Mallory said and shook her head. "And they seem to love him. They wind around his ankles every night when he comes home." She still couldn't believe it, but she supposed she shouldn't have been surprised. Alex could turn every woman to putty. She just hadn't known his powers extended to felines.

Lilli glanced at the other side of the room. "It looks like there's going to be an announcement. We should join our husbands."

Mallory walked to Alex's side. He held a glass of Scotch in his hand and appeared attentive, but relaxed. She knew better, though. He hadn't touched his drink and every once in a while his jaw clenched.

She shouldn't care, and she told herself it was just human nature not to want to see another human being suffer, but Mallory knew that the first wave of her white-hot anger and indignation against Alex had finally cooled. "Are you okay?" she asked in a low voice.

He met her gaze and she saw a flash of turbulence before he covered it. "Yes. You're drinking water. Did you want something else?"

She shook her head, thinking she would just like to leave the oppressive atmosphere. "Who is he?" she asked, nodding toward the man getting ready to speak.

"James Oldham, one of the board of directors," he said.

"He has shifty eyes," she whispered.

Alex chuckled. "You continue to delight me."

His statement was so natural it caught her off guard. Mallory often dismissed Alex's compliments because she assumed a hidden agenda. This time there was none and she couldn't suppress a burst of pleasure.

"Ladies and gentlemen, thank you for joining us on such short notice," James Oldham said. "As you know, Megalos-De Luca Enterprises has long provided travelers all over the world with the ultimate resort luxury experience. We continue to do that. We also continue to refine the bottom line so that we keep our stockholders happy. To best facilitate that continued refinement, we are bringing in the best of the best in reengineering consulting firms to help us improve our financial edge in this complicated world market. Please welcome Damien Medici," he said and the door to the room opened, revealing a tall, dark man with black hair, olive skin and dark, watchful eyes. His lips lifted in the barest of smiles. He turned his head and she glimpsed a jagged scar along his jaw.

Mallory watched Alex give a nod and a soundless clap of his hands while the rest of the room applauded. Max leaned toward Alex and said something. Mallory felt the tension in the room grow exponentially and took a sip of her water.

"No relation to Santa Claus, is he?" she said to Alex.

His lips twisted in humor and he slid his hand behind her back. "Not exactly. He goes by a couple nicknames. The Terminator. Switch for switchblade. Here he comes," he said.

Mallory turned to find Damien Medici studying

the four of them intently, with particular interest in Alex and Max. He extended his hand. "The two namesakes of the company. I've heard much about you. Max, Alex," he said, shaking each of their hands. "We have more in common than you probably think. I look forward to working with you."

Damien turned to Lilli. "Mrs. De Luca?" he enquired and smiled. "Max did well." He then turned to Mallory and extended his hand. "As did Alex, Mrs. Megalos."

Mallory reluctantly accepted his hand. "Mr. Medici," she said.

"I'll be meeting with each of you individually soon," Damien said to Max and Alex.

"Welcome to Megalos-De Luca Enterprises," Alex said in his regular charming voice, but Mallory didn't miss the emphasis on the company name. Alex and Max would protect the company. Damien might not know it, but he would be facing the fight of his life if he wrangled with the two of them.

Damien nodded and walked away. Alex and Max exchanged a look then Alex glanced down, pulling his BlackBerry from his pocket. He frowned. "We should go," he said to Mallory and escorted her from the gathering.

Alex was completely silent during the drive to the condo. That should have been fine, but Mallory couldn't stop herself from being concerned. She knew he was bothered about Damien Medici, but she wondered if there was something else bringing that dark look to his face. Could it be something about the development in West Virginia?

He absently wished her good-night, and Mallory went to bed, but didn't sleep well. Rising early despite her lack of sleep, she showered and got dressed. Entering the kitchen, she was surprised to see Alex seated at the table talking on the phone.

As soon as he caught sight of her, he cut off the conversation. "Please have a seat," he said, standing and pulling out a chair for her.

Mallory felt a ripple of uneasiness. Although she glimpsed slight shadows beneath his eyes, Alex seemed almost too controlled, too calm. She took the seat he offered. "Okay."

He took a deep breath. "I'll give you the divorce you want."

Shock hit her like a cannonball. Surely she hadn't heard him correctly. "Excuse me?"

"I said I'll give you a divorce," he said in that too calm voice.

Shock hit her again, followed by confusion. "I don't understand."

He shoved his hands into his pockets, one sign that he wasn't as calm as he seemed. "I don't expect you to understand. That's why I'm giving you the divorce. Chloe," he began.

"Your ex-girlfriend?" Mallory could hardly forget the woman since the willowy blonde had shown up during her trip to the islands and the wedding reception.

"We were briefly involved, which was a terrible mistake on my part," he said in a cold, crisp voice. "I can't allow you to suffer as a result of my mistake."

Mallory shook her head, still confused. "I don't understand. Would you please sit down? This is a strange enough conversation without my having to crane to look up at you."

Alex reluctantly sat. "Chloe is threatening to go to the press with a story that she's pregnant with my child. She's claiming she got pregnant while you and I were seeing each other."

Mallory's heart stopped. "Oh, my God," she whispered. "She's pregnant with your child?"

He shook his head. "No, she isn't."

"How can you be sure?"

"I always wore protection and we were only together twice," he said.

"But condoms don't provide perfect protection," Mallory said more to herself than to Alex, her mind spinning with the news. She felt a deep twist of resentment and jealousy at the thought of Chloe bearing Alex's child.

"The woman is a pathological liar," Alex said. "I wouldn't be surprised if she's not pregnant at all."

Mallory stared at him. "Really?"

"Really," he said and finally swore. "She showed up uninvited at our wedding reception, for God's sake."

"Were you still seeing her when you and I—"

"Absolutely not," he said and took her hand in his. "I swear it. I broke up with her before you and I got involved. Once there was you, there was no one else."

Mallory felt a shiver run down her body at the naked honesty in Alex's eyes. Her emotions running all over the place, she looked at him helplessly. "If she's lying, then why do you want to divorce me?"

"I can't put you through this kind of scandal. I refuse to do it. You don't deserve it. The only way I can protect you is to divorce you." He drew in a slow breath. "I'll take care of it quickly and quietly. I have to leave town on business for the next few days. While I'm gone you can choose where you'd like to move. I think it's best that you leave Vegas, at least for a while, so you won't have to answer questions." He paused. "I'm sorry. Divorcing you is that last thing I want to do, but it's the only choice. Chloe is promising a long, drawn-out fight, and I know you would never escape the whispers. Chloe was my mistake, not yours. You deserve the fresh start that I can't give you."

Fifteen minutes later, she watched him walk out of the condo. Mallory felt as if she'd been sucked into a killer tornado and spit out in pieces. She wandered the condo, shell-shocked.

She should be happy, shouldn't she? This was what she'd wanted, no, demanded of Alex. Now she could be free to pursue her own life, her own dreams. Freedom was what she'd been craving for years.

Why did she feel like crying? Why did she feel as if someone important to her had died? Biting her lip, Mallory walked to her new bedroom and felt tears stinging her eyes. She blinked furiously to make them stop, but they streamed down her face.

Sinking onto the bed, she tried to come to terms with what Alex had told her and his solution. Her cats hopped onto the bed and rubbed against her. She grabbed Gorgeous and held him against her. He mewed in sympathy.

She glanced at the books for her online class sitting on her dresser. She'd had a hard time concentrating lately. How much harder would it be now?

She tried to formulate a plan. While she packed her belongings, she would figure out where to go. California, she thought, and immediately rejected the idea. Somewhere different. Somewhere that no one knew her. The East Coast. Florida. A remote, sunny island. A downpour of images of the time she and Alex had shared in Cabo stormed through her. The memories were so sweet she ached from them.

She pulled a suitcase from the closet and began to fill it with clothes. Heaven help her, she was confused. She'd spent most of her life doing what everyone else had told her to do. During the last month, she'd been tricked into marrying the man of her dreams. Now she was getting a divorce. She hadn't wanted to get married. She didn't want a divorce.

The thought took her by surprise. She opened

another drawer and dumped the clothes into the suitcase then stopped. A question echoed in her mind, throughout her body. What did she *really* want?

Four days later, Alex returned from his business trip. Riding the elevator to the penthouse, he dreaded walking into his home. He'd been tempted to stay at the resort downtown. Even though Mallory had been furious with him during the last week they'd been together, he'd still looked forward to her presence.

He despised the fact that his life had become tabloid fodder. He despised the fact that he'd been forced to cut Mallory out of his life for her protection. He felt gutted, empty. He'd always been so sure a woman couldn't get to his soul. Until Mallory.

He'd even started liking her cats.

The elevator stopped at the top floor and the doors opened. Swearing under his breath, he braced himself for utter quiet. He opened the door to the condo and gritted his teeth. He had never known he could be this miserable.

Closing the door behind him, he dropped his suitcase in the foyer and walked into the den. The calico sprinted out to greet him with the black male at her heels. He stared at the cats in confusion.

"What the—"

The cats wove around his ankles, mewing. Untangling himself, Alex raced to Mallory's room. Empty except for the furniture that had been there before she moved. His heart fell to his stomach.

Why the hell were the cats here? Had she left them with him for some sick reason? He backtracked to the kitchen, searching for Jean, but there was no sign of the housekeeper. He noticed, however, that the sliding door to the deck was slightly ajar. He stood very still. Was that music playing?

Confusion and anticipation coursed through him. He stepped outside and heard the music coming from the upper deck. He couldn't imagine why she would still be here. He'd made it perfectly clear to Mallory that he would give her a divorce. He hadn't softened the scandal he was facing.

Climbing the stairs to the upper terrace, he didn't know what to expect. It certainly wasn't finding Mallory reclined on a chaise lounge wearing a silky gown.

She glanced up to meet his gaze and smiled. A knot of longing formed in his throat. He wondered if he was dreaming.

"Welcome home," she said and sat up in the chair. "I poured a glass of Scotch for you. It's on the bar if you want it."

He did. Lifting the small glass from the bar, he took a long sip, feeling the burn all the way down. He met her gaze again. "I thought you would be gone."

"I almost was," she said, rising to her feet. "I packed up everything. But the whole time I couldn't stop asking myself what I really wanted." She moved toward him.

His heart pounded hard and deep. "And what was your answer?"

"I want to be the woman of your dreams," she said. "I want to be the woman you choose above all the other women. I want to be the woman you love even though you never thought you would fall in love."

He narrowed his eyes, steeling himself against the temptation to take her in his arms. "Love won't fix the mess with Chloe."

Her eyes flashed with sadness then she lifted her chin in determination. "Do you love me?"

Stunned by her boldness, he stared at her for a full moment before responding. "It doesn't matter. I won't put you through this scandal."

She pressed her lips together. "Afraid I can't take it, right?"

"I didn't say that," he said.

"You may as well. Are you going to underestimate me like everyone else has?"

Surprised again, Alex felt as if she were taking him on a ride with hairpin turns and gut-wrenching drops. "I don't underestimate you. I know you're an amazing woman. Adventurous, kind, sexy."

She made a moue of her lips. "Sounds like you might like me a little bit."

"A little bit," he echoed and swore. He took

another swallow of his drink. He didn't know how it had happened, but he was tied up in knots over her.

"I wouldn't have thought you were the quitting kind," she said. "Not if it was something you really wanted."

"I'm not," he said.

"Then you must not want me very much," she said.

His breath left his body. "Dammit," he said reaching for her. "I want you too much. I can't stand to see you hurt by all this. I finally find a woman who makes me feel like a human being, who makes me feel alive inside and I have to give her up. Dammit, it's killing me, Mallory. Don't make it any harder."

Mallory blinked, dropping her jaw and working it for a few seconds. She shook her head. "I'm going to make it very hard. I love you and I'm tired of being told what I should want and what I should do. You and I got married and I can stomp my foot and scream and rail at you because of the deal you made with my father, but the truth is I wouldn't have married you if I didn't want to." She took a deep breath. "And I don't think anyone, including my father, could have forced you to marry me. So, Mr. Megalos, consider yourself stuck with me."

Alex stared at her in amazement, not quite able to believe her. "Are you sure? This is going to get messy."

"Life is messy," she said. "I want to spend mine with you."

In that moment she made all Alex's dreams come

true at once. He pulled her against him. "I love you more than I can tell you. You really are the woman of my dreams."

He took her mouth in a soul-searing kiss that went on and on. He felt dampness against his cheeks and realized she was crying. Pulling back, he searched her face. "Mallory?"

"I was so afraid," she said. "So afraid that maybe I was wrong, that maybe you didn't love me."

"Oh, sweetheart," he said, pulling her against him. "I guess I'll just have to spend the rest of my life telling you and showing you how very much I love you."

She took a trembling breath. "Starting now?"

He swung her into his arms and headed down the steps. "Starting now."

Epilogue

Six weeks later…

Poring over lists, charts and plans for Alex's resort in West Virginia, Mallory sneaked a peek through the glass oven door and felt a twinge of relief. Good, she hadn't burned anything this time. Cooking wasn't her forte, and even though it wasn't technically necessary for her to cook, she wanted to be able to fix something special for Alex. He'd been working so hard, engaged in a constant corporate battle with Damien Medici. The master of reorganization had been a major pain in the rear and she just wished he would go far, far away. The planet Jupiter sounded like a good place for him.

With both her kitties snoozing at her feet, she glanced back at her work. She took her job for Alex very seriously. In fact, Alex joked that she took it too seriously sometimes when she was glued to her cell phone getting answers to questions and smoothing out rough spots. She could tell, however, that he was proud of her. It was amazing how much their relationship had changed once they'd admitted their love to each other. The difference was night and day.

Hearing the front door open, she watched the cats race out of the room. Seconds later they began to mew in welcome.

"Good afternoon, you spoiled, beautiful felines," Alex said in an affectionate voice at odds with his words. "What have you been up to today? Shredding curtains, ripping upholstery? Mallory?" he called.

Her heart still hiccupped at the sound of his voice. "In the kitchen," she said, rising from the table and peeking into the oven again. So far, so good.

Alex strode into the room and pulled her into his arms. If she didn't know better, she would say he was even more gorgeous than the first day she'd seen him. "How was your day?" he asked. "Tell me you're finished with your work," he said before she could answer, and lowered his mouth to hers.

Mallory bubbled with laughter, then sank into his kiss and his embrace. He kissed her as if she were the only woman on earth, and she was starting to believe that maybe she was for him.

She pulled back and took a couple of quick breaths. "I had one more thing I wanted to do before—"

"No," he said, shaking his head. "You're done. I have plans for you."

She wondered what was behind the mysterious glint in his green eyes. "Really?"

"I do, and there'll be no stalling, no excuses due to homework or anything else," he said firmly and paused a half-beat. "What is that amazing smell?"

Mallory smiled. "Apple pie. I made it myself. And we have ice cream."

His gaze softened. "You didn't have to do that. You could ask the cook—"

"I know. I wanted to." She glanced over his shoulder. "Time to take it out," she said, and pulled the pie from the oven and set it on a hot pad. "You've been working so hard lately in so many ways," she said, her mind drifting to the problems with Chloe. "I thought you deserved a little treat."

He came up behind her and put his arms around her waist. "We may have to take the pie with us. I've arranged for a celebration."

She turned in his arms and searched his face. "Why? Did Damien move to the other side of the world?"

Alex's face hardened. "No, but he's taking some time away from Megalos-De Luca to handle a crisis somewhere else." He gave a deep sigh. "My good news is that Chloe submitted to a pregnancy test and she's not pregnant."

Relief washed over Mallory. She knew how much Alex had suffered over this. "She can't threaten to sue you anymore."

"Exactly. So I've decided to celebrate by getting your passport stamped."

Mallory dropped her mouth in amazement. "How? When?"

"Tonight," he said. "We'll take my personal jet. We can sleep or do other things on the way," he said in a suggestive voice. "We'll take the pie with us, too."

Mallory's mind flew in a half-dozen different directions. "But I really do have a paper due and I've got to stay on top of those people in West Virginia or they won't get things done the way they should—"

Alex placed his index finger over her mouth. "This is part one of our honeymoon. We're gong to Paris."

"Paris," she echoed. "I've never been."

His lips curved in sexy *gotcha* smile. "I know. I see it as my personal duty to fill up all the pages in your passport the same way I fill up…"

Her face flaming at his intimate suggestion, she covered his mouth with her hand.

He kissed her fingers. "Not blushing, are you?" he teased.

"Stop it. You're making it hard for me to think straight."

He lowered his mouth to a breath away from hers. "One of my other jobs," he said.

She groaned. "Part one. Why did you say this is part one of our honeymoon?"

"Because numbers are infinite," he said, his face turning solemn. "They go on forever. The same way our love will."

"Pinch me," she said. "I can't believe I'm this lucky. Pinch me."

Alex shook his head. "Wait until I get you on the plane. I'll do a lot more pleasurable things than pinch you."

Mallory sighed as he kissed her. She knew he would deliver on his promise. Loving Alex and being loved by him would be the greatest adventure of her life.

* * * * *

The Colton family is back!
Enjoy a sneak preview of
COLTON'S SECRET SERVICE
by Marie Ferrarella,
part of
THE COLTONS: FAMILY FIRST *miniseries.*

Available from Silhouette Romantic Suspense
in September 2008.

He cautioned himself to be leery. He was human and he'd been conned before. But never by anyone nearly so attractive. Never by anyone he'd felt so attracted to.

In her defense, Nick supposed that Georgie could actually be telling him the truth. That she was a victim in all this. He had his people back in California checking her out, to make sure she was who she said she was and had, as she claimed, not even been near a computer but on the road these last few months that the threats had been made.

In the meantime, he was doing his own checking out. Up close and exceedingly personal. So personal he could feel his blood stirring.

It had been a long time since he'd thought of himself as anything other than a law enforcement agent of one type or other. But Georgeann Grady made him remember that beneath the oaths he had taken and his devotion to duty, there beat the heart of a man.

A man who'd been far too long without the touch of a woman.

He watched as the light from the fireplace caressed the outline of Georgie's small, trim, jean-clad body as she moved about the rustic living room that could have easily come off the set of a Hollywood Western. Except that it was genuine.

As genuine as she claimed to be?

Something inside of him hoped so.

He wasn't supposed to be taking sides. His only interest in being here was to guarantee Senator Joe Colton's safety as the latter continued to make his bid for the presidency. Everything else was supposed to be secondary, but, Nick had to silently admit, that was just a wee bit hard to remember right now.

Earlier, before she'd put her precocious handful of a daughter to bed, Georgie had fed his appetite by whipping up some kind of a delicious concoction out of the vegetables she'd pulled from her garden. Vegetables that, by all rights, should have been withered and dried. She'd mentioned that a friend came by on occasion to weed and tend it. Still, it surprised him that somehow she'd managed to make something mouthwatering out of it.

Almost as mouthwatering as she looked to him right at this moment.

Again, he was reminded of the appetite that hadn't been fed, hadn't been satisfied.

And wasn't going to be, Nick sternly told himself. At least not now. Maybe later, when things took on a more definite shape and all the questions in his head were answered to his satisfaction, there would be time to explore this feeling. This woman. But not now.

Damn it.

"Sorry about the lack of light," Georgie said, breaking into his train of thought as she turned around to face him. If she noticed the way he was looking at her, she gave no indication. "But I don't see a point in paying for electricity if I'm not going to be here. Besides, Emmie really enjoys camping out. She likes roughing it."

"And you?" Nick asked, moving closer to her, so close that a whisper would have trouble fitting in. "What do you like?"

The very breath stopped in Georgie's throat as she looked up at him.

"I think you've got a fair shot of guessing that one," she told him softly.

* * * * *

Be sure to look for
COLTON'S SECRET SERVICE
and the other following titles from
THE COLTONS: FAMILY FIRST *miniseries:*

RANCHER'S REDEMPTION
by Beth Cornelison
THE SHERIFF'S AMNESIAC BRIDE
by Linda Conrad
SOLDIER'S SECRET CHILD
by Caridad Piñeiro
BABY'S WATCH
by Justine Davis
A HERO OF HER OWN
by Carla Cassidy

Romantic
SUSPENSE

**Sparked by Danger,
Fueled by Passion.**

The Coltons Are Back!

Marie Ferrarella
Colton's Secret Service

The Coltons: Family First

On a mission to protect a senator, Secret Service agent
Nick Sheffield tracks down a threatening message only
to discover Georgie Gradie Colton, a rodeo-riding single
mom, who insists on her innocence. Nick is instantly
taken with the feisty redhead, but vows not to let his
feelings interfere with his mission. Now he must figure
out if this woman is conning him or if he can trust her
and the passion they share….

Available September wherever books are sold.

**Look for upcoming Colton titles
from Silhouette Romantic Suspense:**

RANCHER'S REDEMPTION by Beth Cornelison, Available October
THE SHERIFF'S AMNESIAC BRIDE by Linda Conrad, Available November
SOLDIER'S SECRET CHILD by Caridad Piñeiro, Available December
BABY'S WATCH by Justine Davis, Available January 2009
A HERO OF HER OWN by Carla Cassidy, Available February 2009

Visit Silhouette Books at www.eHarlequin.com SRS27598

REQUEST YOUR FREE BOOKS!

**2 FREE NOVELS
PLUS 2
FREE GIFTS!**

Passionate, Powerful, Provocative!

YES! Please send me 2 FREE Silhouette Desire® novels and my 2 FREE gifts (gifts are worth about $10). After receiving them, if I don't wish to receive any more books, I can return the shipping statement marked "cancel". If I don't cancel, I will receive 6 brand-new novels every month and be billed just $4.05 per book in the U.S. or $4.74 per book in Canada, plus 25¢ shipping and handling per book and applicable taxes, if any*. That's a savings of almost 15% off the cover price! I understand that accepting the 2 free books and gifts places me under no obligation to buy anything. I can always return a shipment and cancel at any time. Even if I never buy another book, the two free books and gifts are mine to keep forever.   225 SDN ERVX 326 SDN ERVM

Name	(PLEASE PRINT)

Address	Apt. #

City	State/Prov.	Zip/Postal Code

Signature (if under 18, a parent or guardian must sign)

Mail to the **Silhouette Reader Service:**
IN U.S.A.: P.O. Box 1867, Buffalo, NY 14240-1867
IN CANADA: P.O. Box 609, Fort Erie, Ontario L2A 5X3

Not valid to current subscribers of Silhouette Desire books.

Want to try two free books from another line?
Call 1-800-873-8635 or visit www.morefreebooks.com.

* Terms and prices subject to change without notice. N.Y. residents add applicable sales tax. Canadian residents will be charged applicable provincial taxes and GST. Offer not valid in Quebec. This offer is limited to one order per household. All orders subject to approval. Credit or debit balances in a customer's account(s) may be offset by any other outstanding balance owed by or to the customer. Please allow 4 to 6 weeks for delivery. Offer available while quantities last.

Your Privacy: Silhouette Books is committed to protecting your privacy. Our Privacy Policy is available online at www.eHarlequin.com or upon request from the Reader Service. From time to time we make our lists of customers available to reputable third parties who may have a product or service of interest to you. If you would prefer we not share your name and address, please check here. ☐

Silhouette *Desire*

Gifts from a Billionaire

JOAN HOHL

THE M.D.'S MISTRESS

Dr. Rebecca Jameson collapses from
exhaustion while working at a remote
African hospital. Fellow doctor Seth Andrews
ships her back to America so she can heal.
Rebecca is finally with the sexy surgeon
she's always loved. But would their affair
last longer than the week?

**Available September
wherever books are sold.**

Always Powerful, Passionate and Provocative.

COMING NEXT MONTH

#1891 PRINCE OF MIDTOWN—Jennifer Lewis
Park Avenue Scandals
This royal had only one way to keep his dedicated—and lovely—
assistant under his roof...seduce her into his bed!

#1892 THE M.D.'S MISTRESS—Joan Hohl
Gifts from a Billionaire
Finally she was with the sexy surgeon she'd always loved. But
would their affair last longer than the week?

#1893 BABY BONANZA—Maureen Child
Billionaires and Babies
Secret twin babies? A carefree billionaire discovers he's a
daddy—but is he ready to become a groom?

#1894 WED BY DECEPTION—Emilie Rose
The Payback Affairs
The husband she'd believed dead was back—and very much alive.
And determined to make her his...at any cost.

#1895 HIS EXPECTANT EX—Catherine Mann
The Landis Brothers
The ink was not yet dry on their divorce papers when she
discovered she was pregnant. Could a baby bring them a second
chance?

#1896 THE DESERT KING—Olivia Gates
Throne of Judar
Forced to marry to save his throne, this desert king could not deny
the passion he felt for his bride of *in*convenience.

SDCNM0808